"You men seem so easy to shock . . ."

Cynthia Morton rolled into a kneeling position beside Longarm. "I can't help doing whatever feels natural, no matter what Queen Victoria may feel about so-called crimes against nature."

Longarm hissed in pleasure as she began to demonstrate her ability to shock. Aside from it being a statute felony in more than one state, including Colorado, she did it shockingly well . . .

Longarm groaned aloud, "It's a good thing I'm a *federal* lawman."

→•← TABOR EVANS →•←

LONGARM

AND THE HANGMAN'S VENGEANCE

J
JOVE BOOKS, NEW YORK

LONGARM AND THE HANGMAN'S VENGEANCE

A Jove Book/published by arrangement with
the author

PRINTING HISTORY
Jove edition/February 1988

ISBN: 0-515-09445-5

Jove Books are published by The Berkley Publishing Group,
200 Madison Avenue, New York, New York 10016.
The name "JOVE" and the "J" logo
are trademarks belonging to Jove Publications, Inc.

PRINTED IN THE UNITED STATES OF AMERICA

10 9 8 7 6 5 4 3 2 1

Chapter 1

The Denver sky was blushing a handsome shade of dusty rose as the neighbor kids were enjoying a cheerful-sounding game of kick the can. U.S. Marshal William Vail, taking in the sights of the summer evening, let his belt out a couple of notches and lowered his considerable behind to the steps of his veranda, hoping to light his after-supper cigar without getting fussed at.

The freshly lit smoke tasted just right after chicken, dumplings, and cherry pie, no matter what his old woman thought of his favorite brand; she was always fussing at him for sitting out on the step in his shirt sleeves, as well. But he figured he was just as sedate as that fool neighbor lady who let her daughters play with boys right out in the middle of Sherman Avenue. Gals hadn't been allowed to behave so freely back when he was young.

The pudgy, middle-aged lawman's evening reverie didn't last as long as he'd hoped it might. For sure enough, coming along the sandstone walk at a grim pace was his senior deputy, Custis Long from West-by-God-Virginia, and anyone could see he was mighty pissed about something.

Vail was all too sure he knew what it was, as the somewhat younger and considerably taller and leaner figure wearing a pancaked Stetson and tweed suit of matching tobacco-brown bore down on him. But all Vail said was, "Evening, Longarm. We can't chicken and dumpling you no more, but there's plenty of coffee and at least a couple of slices of pie left inside."

Longarm said he'd just eaten, sat down beside his boss, and got out a three-for-a-nickel cheroot as he said, "I just read the duty roster. You'd left for the day before that prissy clerk of yours dared to post it."

One of the kids out front kicked the can galley-west, and as it rattled and tinkled along the tree-shaded avenue Billy Vail said, "They didn't have tin cans when I was that age. You?"

Longarm shook his head and replied, "There was an old lady over in another hollow, back home, who preserved apples and such in jars. She was rumored to be a witch. But nobody went in for tin cans much before the war, and after it I was a mite old for the game them kids is playing." After a pause, he said, "I noticed some damn fool assigned me to a deathwatch at the House of Detention, Billy."

Vail took a drag on his cigar and recited, "A canner, exceedingly canny, one day did remark to his granny, a canner can can anything that one can, but a canner can't can a can, can he?"

Longarm didn't even smile. "Deathwatch is a mighty chickenshit detail for a deputy with six or eight years seniority, ain't it?"

Vail nodded soberly and replied, "It ain't the sort of chore any deputy would volunteer for. I picked you and Guilfoyle because the only others I can spare would be

2

Smiley and Dutch, and the U.S. Constitution forbids cruel and unusual punishment."

"Damn it, Billy, you know they cleared old Dutch for gunning that prisoner."

Vail shrugged. "I promised the boys down at the Federal House of Detention that the execution of the Great Costello was all theirs, come morning. I know I can count on you and Deputy Guilfoyle to see the rascal to the gallows alive and well. Considering the Great Costello's rep, it ain't the sort of chore I'd pick less than the best for."

"I recall reading something about the case in the *Post*, but I'd have paid more attention if I'd known you expected me to kiss the son of a bitch good-bye. How come they call him the Great Costello, anyway? It sounds more like what a vaudeville performer would call himself than the name of a train robber."

"That's on account of him being both," Vail replied. "The Great Costello and his act was enjoying a slow season up in Leadville when they took it in their fool heads to finance further travels by knocking off a silver shipment destined for the Denver Mint."

"I knew why it was a federal case. Killing that federal guard was not the sort of move a man might have wanted to make unless he enjoyed the feel of federal hemp around his neck. But hell, Billy, they picked up the silly son of a bitch within days and—"

"He escaped," Vail cut in. "That wasn't in the *Post* because they caught him again within hours. Then he escaped again. Plural. Twice in the same damned day. Don't ask me how—they're *still* working on it. As an outlaw he's a pathetic greenhorn, but as an escape artist he's a whirling wonder. That's what he was on the vaudeville stage, an escape artist. His boast was that there wasn't a rope, a chain, or a set of shackles as could hold him."

Vail took another drag on his cigar and continued

3

with a weary sigh, "He wasn't just whistling Dixie. He'd been amusing the boys down to the House of Detention by letting 'em put him in cuffs and leg irons, just so they could watch him bust loose."

Longarm frowned thoughtfully and growled, "Hold on, are we talking about our own government issue restraints, not tricky cuffs and such from a magic shop?"

Vail nodded his head and said, "I told you we were working on how he does it. It's sort of discouraging to watch a man slip off cold steel the taxpayers of these United States paid good money for. He can't get out of his patent cell, though. At least, not while an armed guard is posted just outside the bars twenty-four hours a day. But he's still made 'em nervous enough to request our extra help in getting him from the cell to the gallows out back."

Longarm snorted in disgust. "Oh, for God's sake, it ain't that far."

"That's why I'm likely to cloud up and rain all over you and Guilfoyle if the Great Costello don't make such a modest trip, Longarm. The prisoner is a killer, but gutless enough to act docile with a gun trained on him from close range. They'll have his hands cuffed behind him before he leaves the cell, of course, but knowing him, that may not make much difference. You have our permit to blow his spine in two if he makes even one suspicious move on his way out and up. That's why you're it—you know damned well what Dutch or even Smiley would make of such orders if the poor cuss even farted on his way to the gallows."

"I wish I wasn't so damned reliable. I never signed up with the Justice Department to be a hangman, damn it."

Vail said, soothingly, "They got 'em a volunteer for that job. Your job is over the moment you deliver the cuss to the tender mercies of the executioner and his crew, on the platform. If the Great Costello makes one

4

of his great escapes once they have the hood and rope on him, it ain't our necks we have to worry about."

Longarm blew smoke from both nostrils like an angry bull and said, "I still don't like it. I don't mind killing in the line of duty, but no matter what you say about my rough approach to justice from time to time, I'll thank you to recall that I've seldom so much as wounded a gent who wasn't in a position to do me just as dirty. The notion of prodding a helpless man to his death with my gun leaves a mighty bad taste in my mouth, even before I've done it."

"The federal employee Costello killed can't taste nothing, right now," Vail said. "They're fixing to hang him at six A.M. sharp. That means we want you and Guilfoyle down there no later than four in the morning. If I was you, I'd turn in early and set my alarm for, oh, say three?"

Longarm got back to his feet as he replied, "You ain't me, and I'd rather stay up all night than wake up at three in the damned morning to go to a hanging."

Vail shrugged and said, "What you do on your own time between now and then is up to you and her. But make sure she lets you out of bed in time to give the boys a hand. I mean that, old son. If you mess up you can commend your soul to Jesus, for your ass will belong to me."

Chapter 2

Despite Billy Vail's unseemly suggestion, Longarm did not head on down Sherman Avenue to the residence of a certain widow woman—one who would have been more than willing to help him kill the rest of the night. Longarm was too fond of her to subject her to a three A.M. wake-up call after she'd acted so fond of him. Aside from that, he was feeling more morose than horny, even this early. He knew he'd be feeling worse before the long night's vigil was over.

He'd lied to Billy Vail about having eaten earlier. Now he wished he had, so he stopped at a beanery on Larimer Street to put some lining in his stomach. They'd always made *chili con carne* hot enough for him before, but this evening it tasted like spitballs in library paste. The black coffee he washed it down with tasted weak and watery as well, but he drank a couple of extra cups anyway; he knew what a long night he was facing.

As he strolled on toward the federal lockup further downtown, Longarm tried to tell himself this wasn't really the way it had been facing a predawn assault as a teen-aged soldier. It wasn't him, this time, wondering if the next sunrise he would see might be his last. It was the cuss in the death cell, yonder, who should be thinking thoughts like that. Where in the constitution did it say a man who was only stuck with watching a man die was supposed to feel like he was dying too?

It was darker but still too early to suit Longarm when he got to the Federal House of Detention near the Burlington yards. A long freight was pulling out, moaning wistfully about faraway places. Longarm knew the condemned man inside could hear it as well. It was a sound that made a man feel like traveling even when he had no desperate need to be elsewhere.

A seedy little yellow-brick hotel stood across the street from the lockup. Longarm recalled the taproom opening off the lobby. Right now he needed a drink more than he needed a gander at a man with less than twelve hours to live, so that's where he headed.

Once in the dimly lit lobby, Longarm discovered other minds seemed to be running in the same channels. Reporter Crawford of the *Post* was seated in one corner with a schooner of beer and a handsome redhead. He was wearing a checked suit and silly straw hat. The gal's summer-weight suit was a more sensible beige, but her straw boater was even sillier, and she had a press pass stuck in the brim, with a dead hummingbird sort of peeking over the cardboard.

A couple of other local reporters Longarm knew well enough to howdy had taken up other positions under the potted paper palms. But none of them were handsome redheads, so Longarm ambled over to his pal from the *Post* to ask how one got a beer served in the lobby. Crawford raised his and said, "You have to carry 'em out from the taproom. Oh, I'd like you to meet Miss Cynthia Morton from the *Kansas City Star*." Then, of course, he had to tell the redhead who Longarm was,

8

and of course she had to say, "Oh, I've heard so much about you, Marshal Long! Is it true you once traded shots with Jesse James in the flesh?"

Longarm sighed and replied, "I'm only a deputy marshal, and I warned Ned Buntline what I'd do to him if he ever used my name in one of his wild west magazines again."

Then he ticked his hat brim at her and added, "I'd best see if they serve needled beer here to junior grade lawmen. Could I fetch you something more seemly from the bar, ma'am?"

She dimpled up at him and said, "No, thanks. As I was just saying to Mr. Crawford, I hate to start early on a night like this."

"She's a sob sister," Crawford explained, with an owlish wink that indicated he didn't share her reservations about getting drunk early while on deathwatch.

She shot her fellow reporter an annoyed little smile and told Longarm, "I'm no such thing. It's only natural that my readers expect a reporter of my gender to, well, play up the human interest a bit more."

Longarm allowed that sounded fair and excused himself to go get that beer. As he approached the taproom doorway Deputy Guilfoyle came out with two schooners, grinned at Longarm, and said, "I figured on meeting you here. You wanna get laid?"

Longarm smiled thinly and replied, "That's mighty considerate of you, but, no offense, you just ain't my type."

Guilfoyle laughed. "I've never been that desperate, neither. I'm talking about women. I got me one upstairs too damned pretty to have escaped from the pages of the Police Gazette, and she says she has a friend."

"Male or female?" asked Longarm, warningly. So the young and somewhat goofy-looking Guilfoyle explained, "They're staying here at the hotel. Ain't met both yet. Met the one I'm taking these suds to just a few

9

minutes ago. She said her pal was too shy to drink in public without no escort. When I asked her how shy *she* might be, she allowed we'd both be more respectable if we got drunk together in her room, so—"

"I know how lonesome ladies lure us into such temptations," Longarm cut in. "Just make sure you meet me across the street no later than four, and try to get there sober enough to stand up."

Guilfoyle grinned knowingly and said, "Getting drunk wasn't exactly the vice I had in mind. You sure you don't want us to fix you up with her pard, old pard?"

Longarm hesitated, then he shook his head and said, "One of us oughta keep track of the time. What room will I find you in if you don't?"

"214. I'd best get on up and see how lucky this night turns out for me. No shit, she's really good looking and, so far, she ain't mentioned money even once."

Longarm laughed, told him the night was still young, and let him pass.

The taproom was more crowded than the lobby; the hotel wasn't big enough to hold that many guests. Longarm recognized some other reporters as well as some of the courthouse gang. It looked as if the Great Costello was going to have quite an audience for his last command performance. But at the rate the boys were drinking to him, this early, it seemed doubtful many of them would be able to report, or care, how well the hanging went.

Longarm elbowed his belly to the bar, and once he caught the barmaid's eye, ordered a pitcher instead of a schooner. For she was pretty, and knew it, and there was just no telling if and when a man who wasn't proposing marriage might be able to catch her eye again.

As she filled his awesome order for him a blue-uniformed gent next to Longarm said, "I should have thought of that. It takes so long between drinks tonight

10

that a man can sober up from one afore he gets the next."

Longarm recognized the badge on the visored cap above the somewhat flushed face. "I take it you just come off duty, across the way?"

The guard said, "Nope. I ain't reported in yet. That's how come I'm drinking so serious. Got to hang a man in the morning and I just hate to do that, even drunk."

"I know the feeling. I'm one of the boys you sent for from the marshal's office. It would hardly be fair of me to lecture you on the evils of Demon Rum on such an occasion, but are you all right, old son?"

The guard shrugged and answered, "No. I got to hang a man in the morning. But I'll be there with bells on, if that's what you mean."

Longarm didn't answer. The gent was old enough to vote and it was up to every such man to judge for himself whether he needed a drink, and how often. So Longarm paid for his big drink, tipping the sass more than she was worth, if less than she might think she had coming, and headed back to the lobby.

The redhead was still seated in the corner, but Crawford's overstuffed chair was empty. When Longarm joined her, Cynthia Morton stared at the pitcher in Longarm's hand as if she'd never seen one before and said, "Mr. Crawford just left."

Longarm sat in the vacant chair, saying, "I noticed. Did he say where he was going, ma'am?"

"No. As a matter of fact, he just leaped to his feet and dashed off without a word. Didn't you see him just now in the taproom?"

Longarm shook his head and said, "The G.A.R. could be holding a parade in there without attracting all that much attention. He must have been feeling poorly —it ain't like old Crawford to be rude to a lady."

Then he tipped the pitcher to his face to enjoy a sip of suds over the side, as if it were a big schooner. She

11

repressed a grimace and indicated Crawford's abandoned as well as daintier container on a nearby table, asking, "Wouldn't you feel, well, less clumsy, if you poured that beer like almost everyone else I know?"

"Not hardly. I learned one time, down Mexico way, how unwise it could be to drink from the same glass a gent who lit out running had just been drinking from. If my uncouth cowboy ways offend you, ma'am, I'll just go drink somewhere else and we'll say no more about it."

But as he shifted his weight as if to rise, she placed a soft restraining hand on his sleeve to implore, "Please don't. I didn't mean to imply you were being uncouth. It's just that . . . my, you must have strong wrists. You handle that big pitcher with no more effort than most men expend on a demitasse."

He took another swig and placed the pitcher to one side as he told her, "I'll try to act more natural. I can see that you ain't enjoying this deathwatch, neither. Maybe if we keep each other company the night won't drag as bad."

"That's just what I was about to say. Mr. Crawford was saying, before he left just now, that you were a sort of diamond in the rough."

Longarm frowned and decided, "I hope he's really sick as a dog, then. I don't see why folk keep saying I'm rough. I was brung up by the Good Book and my ma never served soup unless everyone washed their hands before setting down to table."

For some reason that made her smile. She had a nice way of smiling with her soft, kissy-looking lips. He decided not to push his luck by asking her permission to smoke, though; he suspected she might not be used to three-for-a-nickel cheroots, coming from the big city and all.

That reminded him to ask her why the *Kansas City Star* was all that interested in the dawn death of a half-ass desperado, though he had to put it more delicately. When this seemed to puzzle her, he added, "I don't see how even Ned Buntline could make a wild west owlhoot outta poor old Costello. As far as I know, he only robbed one train and got caught in next to no time. They'd have let him off with ten at hard if he hadn't managed to gun that train guard in the process."

She sighed and said, "He swears he never fired his gun. Maybe one of the others taking part in the robbery with him did that."

Longarm raised an eyebrow at her and asked, "When did he tell you all this?"

"I've interviewed him more than once during his trial, and before that in Kansas City, before he was forced into a life of crime. He was once a famous stage magician, you know."

Longarm reached for his big drink and drank some more before he said, "Nobody can force a grown man to steal, or even beg. I know this because I've been broke and hungry more than once, and neither temptation ever crossed my mind."

"That's different. You're obviously a strong man. You can't expect lesser men to have your strength of character."

"You're wrong," he replied, "that's why I pack a badge. Like I said, it's easy to wind up broke and hungry, and ninety-nine out of a hundred men, women, and children can manage to tough it through without busting the law. My job is to deal with that one who can't, or won't."

"Have you no pity at all for those who simply can't live up to your severe Calvinistic code?" she asked.

He looked incredulous and replied, "Hold on. I know lots of Roman Catholics, Jews, and Mormons who hold it's just plain wrong to kill and steal. Where would we be if we allowed just anyone to bust the laws every time they found the going a mite rough? As for feeling sorry for law busters, of course I feel sorry for 'em. I feel sorry for mad dogs, too, but that don't mean I want 'em running about endangering man or beast."

He helped himself to another swig of needled beer, put the pitcher back down with a weary shrug, and said, "Never mind. In a little while this'll all be over and we'll be able to study on more cheerful matters."

She glanced at the wall clock over the hotel desk, gasped, and said, "Oh, Lord, it's not even ten o'clock yet!"

"I was hoping you wouldn't notice. Time surely is a funny substance, ain't it? An hour spent at something happy don't seem long enough, whilst one minute spent on a hot stove seems far too long. I reckon that right now old Costello feels every hour like it was a minute. Meanwhile, since we ain't watching the clock from his point of view, the hands seem sort of stuck." After a moment of silence, he asked, "You sure I can't get you something to drink, ma'am? Just sitting here another eight or nine hours figures to get sort of tedious."

She shook her head and said, "I may have to sip something strong indeed before we cross over to watch the final moments of poor Mr. Costello, but I have a bottle of something strong indeed in my room, upstairs. I don't think I should go near it before ... six in the morning?"

"It'll be over by then, if things go the way they're meant to. I have to head across even earlier. I'd say your best bet would be to hold out until about five, get drunk as you can, and join us around five-thirty. He'll still be in his cell. It's a short walk to the gallows out back."

She looked sick and said, "I don't think I'm going to be able to make it on my own. Mr. Crawford had agreed to escort me to the execution yard and sort of prop me up if my knees gave way. I don't suppose you—"

"I can't," he cut in. "You reporters and required wit-

14

nesses will be let into the yard to watch, but I fear I'll be up on the platform during the time your knees are most apt to feel the weakest."

She looked at him in sudden horror and asked, "You're not . . . not the one, are you?"

He shook his head and answered quickly, "Lord, no. It's bad enough my sidekick and me have to hand him over to the hangman and his crew. Don't ask me why— or maybe I should ask you why, since you know the poor cuss. Is the Great Costello as good at escaping as they say he is?"

"Well, I've never seen him escape from a gallows yard. But having seen his act more than once I can tell you he's incredible when it comes to escaping from locked steamer trunks and so forth."

Then she laughed in sudden understanding and said, "Mr. Crawford was wondering what you were doing here tonight, since you had no connection with the case. Are you really worried the Great Costello will escape his own hanging, as if he was up on a real stage?"

"I ain't worried about it," Longarm said, "someone else must be. The Great Costello would have to be the bee's knees as an escape artist even without me and Guilfoyle riding herd on him."

"Heavens, I'm forgetting my duties as a reporter," she said. "Let me take some notes as you tell me just what extra precautions you'll be taking in the morning and . . . Oh, dear I left my pad and pencil up in my room, silly me."

As she rose, Longarm got to his own feet, of course, since along with learning to wash up before coming to table, he'd been taught that was the thing to do whenever a lady got up, no matter where she might be heading. So he was mildly surprised when she suggested, "Bring your pitcher along, if you like."

He left it where it was. For if they were just going up to her room for a pad and pencil, there was no need to

15

tote such a cumbersome load, and, if they weren't fixing to come right back down, he didn't want the infernal beer at all.

If he was reading the smoke signals in her warm green eyes at all right, he was going to have a hell of a time making it to the hanging in time, even sober.

Chapter 3

He hadn't been wrong. Being of the female persuasion
—and no doubt feeling this called upon her to display a
good deal more mystification about the simple facts of
human nature than any man—Cynthia stared in wonder
as Longarm struck a match for their second-wind
smoke, and asked him, "How did you do that, speaking
of magicians?"

Since the burning match was the first light they'd had
on the subject for some time, Longarm didn't shake it
out as he got his cheroot going. Gripping the smoke
between his smiling teeth and noting for sure, at last,
that she was red-headed all over, he told her, "It's hard
to say, now that we're feeling a mite sane again."

She blew the match out and snuggled her naked
charms against his love-warmed flank, saying, "You're
right. It was insane. I'm sure I'd have said no if only I'd
known what you were doing before you were, well,
doing it. My God, I'd hate to get into a gunfight with
you. I know it seems a little late now to tell you I'm no

17

blushing schoolgirl, but up until now I've always managed to hold out for the usual flowers, books, and candy for at least a few nights."

He patted her bare shoulder with his free hand and said, "We only had this one night, if you're really heading back to K.C. right after the hanging. I'm sorry about the flowers, books, and candy, but I wasn't expecting to meet nobody but the Great Costello this close to the rail yards."

She laughed softly and began to toy with the hair on his belly as she replied, "I wasn't expecting to meet anyone like you out here, either. But as you must have guessed by now, celibacy is not my style by choice. You must think I'm a mighty easy lay, right?"

He let out some smoke, kissed the part in her hair, and told her, "Don't be too hard on yourself, honey, I'm an easy lay as well. So what do you reckon we ought to do about that, call one another names or just relax and enjoy this happy turn of events?"

She began to spin belly yarn further down as she kissed his naked chest. "I can see my maidenly reservations are falling on deaf ears, thank God. In a way, I'm sort of glad we'll only have this one short night together."

"How come? Are you bored with my efforts to please a lady already?"

She slid her free hand all the way to where they both must have wanted it and gave his flaccid virility a playful squeeze. "You haven't begun to please me if you're half the man I suspect you are. I just meant I was sort of glad we don't really know one another and probably won't meet again, because that way it won't really matter what you think of me, later, if I really let myself go with you, see?"

Longarm felt himself beginning to rise to the occasion as she fondled him with skill and enthusiasm. He took a last drag on the cheroot, reached to snub it out in

18

the ashtray on the bed table, and told her, "I'm game for anything that don't hurt. But, no offense, I got the distinct impression you was letting yourself go when first we started a short spell back, you hot-natured little thing."

She rolled into a kneeling position beside him as she sort of growled, "You're right about my having a passionate nature, Custis. I've often wondered whether it was a blessing or a curse. I've lost one husband and more than one steady boyfriend because you men seem so easy to shock, but I can't help it. I can behave myself in a ladylike fashion if I have to, or I can just let go and do whatever feels natural, no matter what Queen Victoria and her ilk may feel about so-called crimes against nature."

Longarm hissed in pleasure as she began to demonstrate her ability to shock. Aside from it being a statute felony in more than one state, including Colorado, she did it shockingly well.

"It's a good thing I'm a *federal* lawman," he groaned. She didn't answer. She couldn't, with her mouth so full. He protested, "Hold on, let's not waste it." But it was too late as he began to climax from his insteps up. Then she spun on her center of gravity to impale herself on his raging orgasm and, while this left him unable to move for a time, she proceeded to slide up and down as if she were riding a merry-go-round, or rather as if she were a merry-go-round pony setting it's own pace on a brass pole that had no say in the matter.

He couldn't be sure—the room was dark, save for the faint street light through the window curtains—but from the feel of her fingernails between them, he suspected she was playing with herself as well as driving him *loco*. He tried to roll her over to finish, again, right. She gasped, "No. Let me finish this way and then you can do anything you want to me."

That sounded fair. She'd brought herself to climax in

19

such a teasing way he feared for her safety. Then he climaxed, his way, with her on her back and her ankles locked around the nape of his neck.

When he asked her if he'd hurt her she just raised her eager little rump clear of the mattress and told him the man who could hurt her that way was yet to be born. Then she let him roll off again, gasping for breath.

He didn't grope for a smoke this time. She didn't seem to smoke in bed between times—her notion of between times hardly justified striking a match. She must have been thinking about the passage of time, too, for she asked him how much time they had left.

He chuckled fondly, held her closer, and said, "It has to be later than it was when we first agreed to kill the night this way, bless your sweet hide. But sweet as it's been, it can't be that late, yet. You go ahead and fall asleep if you've a mind to. I can't, but I'd be proud to wake you up when I got to leave, hear?"

She snuggled closer and replied, "I'm not the least bit sleepy. Every time I cool off a bit I can't help think-ing about that poor wretch they'll be hanging at dawn."

He grimaced in the dark and said, "The law and Mother Nature don't agree on the hour of dawn, pre-cise. At this latitude, in high summer, the sun will be well up by six A.M. That's why I don't have to keep groping for my watch. The sky outside ought to be pearling gray by four. I can get there as late as four-thirty if you're still feeling this friendly when the grim time comes for me to go."

She sighed. "Damn, I wish it could be at least sort of dark when they do it. I never asked for this assignment and I've never seen a hanging before."

"I have. It's worst when it's done informal, but you won't see nothing that awful, come morning. They'll have a black hood covering his face and once the trap springs he'll drop out of sight entire."

"I fear I've too vivid an imagination to see just surface images," she said. "I confess that when I first met you, downstairs, I was able to picture you with your pants off, quite accurately, as it turned out."

He chuckled and told her, "I could tell how you was built without your duds on, too, albeit you turned out a mite more athletic than any man has a right to dream."

She kissed his shoulder and insisted, "I just know I'm going to be able to read the tortured expression on that poor man's face, no matter how they cover it, and when he drops down to the end of that awful rope. . . . Tell me something, dear, is it true what they say about a hanged man dying with an erection?"

He laughed and replied, "I might have known you'd be interested in a thing like that. Save for a few Indians, most of the gents I've seen dying that way had their pants on. But I have it on the authority of an army undertaker that it depends a lot on whether they die slow or sudden. Slow strangulation raises the blood pressure and other matters. The Great Costello is getting a first class hanging by a professional crew, so he'll likely die more dignified than a Cheyenne renegade I recalls with some disgust."

He didn't think she wanted to know that, either way, they always voided their bladders and often shit their pants, so he didn't mention it.

Still, she said, "It seems so cruel. I won't argue with you that he went astray and deserves to be punished, but he swears he wasn't the one who shot that guard who surprised them in the act of, well, an act. He says nobody would have been hurt, or even known about that robbery, if things had gone the way he planned."

"The Northfield Raid didn't go the way the James-Younger gang planned. One of the innocent bystanders killed that day was only in his teens. Cole Younger was lucky as hell to get off with life at hard. Had I been his judge, he'd have swung for certain. I don't know as much about the Great Costello's botched robbery, but

21

the law says that it don't matter who pulls the trigger. That cuss they're fixing to hang in the morning had his chance to turn state's evidence if he wanted to say who done the deed. But he hung tough with the federal prosecutor, refusing to name even one other member of his fool gang, and so now they're hanging him alone, and if he don't like it, tough."

"Brrr," she said. "I like you better when you're talking about a lady's tits. I think I need some of that nerve medication I was talking about earlier. Let me up, the bottle's in my overnight bag, under the bed."

He didn't argue as she rolled away from him, sat on the edge of the bed, and bent over to fish a bottle of whatever from her luggage. The view might have been even more inspiring if the room had been lighter. When she sat up, he heard a cork popping in a way that suggested she might have been steadying her nerves earlier. Then she gurgled an amazing swig for such a petite person, neat, before she half turned and held the bottle out to him, asking, "Won't you join me? It's not wise for a lady to drink alone in the company of a naked gentleman. He might take advantage of her."

Longarm laughed, took the bottle, and sniffed the muzzle before he protested. "Thunderation, this stuff is pure corn squeezings, over a hundred proof."

"I think I have a water pitcher on my washstand in the corner if you can't take Kansas corn neat, dear."

"It ain't that I'm a sissy. Like I said when I left that pitcher of beer behind, a man can enjoy his women neat, or he can drink late at night on an empty gut. He can't do both." Then he handed the bottle back and said, "You go on and knock yourself out if you want. I got to stay wide awake."

She laughed, put the white lightning away, and they stayed wide awake indeed for quite a spell.

Chapter 4

The atmosphere of the Mile High city was too thin to hold heat through the night, even in high summer. So it was a mite cold as well as sort of gray outside when the fully dressed Longarm kissed the naked Cynthia Morton a fond farewell in her open doorway, and promised he'd see her to the Union Depot, after the hanging.

Her kiss was warm enough, but her green eyes were troubled as she shook her head and told him, "I think we'd better quit while we're ahead, dear. It was grand, but I do have a reputation to consider and—"

"Say no more," he interrupted. "My boss will likely be expecting me at the office early, for a change. You see, he's sure to think he knows where I've been all night."

She dimpled up at him, sighed, and said, "God, the things I have to do for the *Kansas City Star*. Please don't flirt with me at the hanging, Custis." Then she shut the door in his face.

He shrugged, turned away, and as he passed Room

23

214 hit the door with his fist and called out, "Up and at 'em, Guilfoyle." Then he went downstairs, through the lobby, and across to the federal lockup.

He'd been worried about being a mite late, but as he entered the guard room he saw he was just as likely too early. A pair of uniformed guards playing checkers across an empty chair glanced up as he entered. Another gent wearing civilian duds put aside the magazine he'd been reading to ask Longarm if he was the hangman. Longarm shook his head and said, "Not hardly. I'm from the marshal's office. My sidekick ought to be along any minute, and you have the advantage on me, Mister . . ?"

"Wagner, Orville Wagner, of the railroad-dicking Wagners," the slightly older man explained. "I'm only here on behalf of the Denver & Rio Grande. The Great Costello scared the shit out of us with that razzle-dazzle that almost worked. I'm here to make sure he won't ever scare us like that no more. They was sort of hoping I could get him to tell us how he did some of it, too, but every time I try to get him to talk he shows me a damned old coin trick."

One of the checker-playing guards chuckled and said, "He sure is an entertaining prisoner. We've strip-searched him over and over and he still makes coins appear outta thin air."

Wagner growled, "If they'd only give me a few minutes alone with the sassy son of a bitch I'd get more than fool coin tricks out of him. Thanks to the sissy views you feds have about such methods, the son of a bitch is fixing to take a mess of secrets with him in a little while."

Longarm nodded soberly and said, "Don't take it so hard. I got a swell confession out of an owlhoot one time without messing him up enough to matter. But the judge wouldn't let us use it against him in court—you know how picky federal courts can be." Then he shot a

24

questioning glance at the guard and added, "I may as well have a look at him before they hood his fool face, if it's all the same to you boys."

One of the guards jumped a black checker with his red, laughed, and said, "Sure, go on back, Longarm. Our other boys are watching him too close for you to torture him serious."

Longarm nodded and, knowing the way, strolled back to the cell blocks. Business had been slow of late, so most of the cells were empty. He found the cell he was looking for easily enough. A coal-oil lamp was burning on a box near a portly guard seated just outside the bars, with a sawed-off ten guage resting across his fat thighs. His bullet head was lowered as close to his chest as the folds of his fat neck allowed. His eyes were closed. When Longarm howdied him, a sardonic voice said softly, "Don't wake him up. He just now fell asleep."

Longarm moved closer. He nodded to the short, shirt-sleeved figure standing inside the death cell and said, "I'm deputy Marshal Custis Long. It would be sort of dumb to ask who you might be."

The condemned man laughed boyishly and replied, "The Great Costello, at your service," and did a funny little dance he'd no doubt done on many a vaudeville stage, offering Longarm a full view of him, front, sides and back. Longarm wasn't too impressed. He'd already been told the showman-turned-train-robber was sort of runty, and he was skinny as well. There was a hint of wiry strength in his almost girlish figure. The small hands attached to more muscular wrists likely accounted for some of the amazing things he was supposed to be able to do with handcuffs. The escape artist's face was more masculine, or maybe just careworn. His black hair was starting to thin at the temples, leaving a sharp V hairline, and his face was a series of Vs from there on down. His heavy eyebrows formed a shallower but sort

25

of satanic V, and his dark eyes swept up at the outer corners in an almost oriental way. His mouth was either smiling all the time or just another natural V. His jaw, a mite developed for such a small-boned gent, was of course another V.

When he saw Longarm didn't seem amused by his flourishes, the Great Costello calmed down and asked what time it was.

Longarm hauled out his pocketwatch, held the dial to the dim light, and said, "Going on quarter after. Now, before we wake this other gent up, would you like to hand over the key or do I have to order a strip-search at gunpoint?"

The Great Costello sighed, reached above his own head, and materialized a key from thin air, asking, "How did you know?"

As Longarm took the key back he replied, "Lucky guess. It's a good notion to sit farther back from the bars when you can't stay awake on guard." Then he tried the key in the lock, smiled despite himself, and added, "Now I want you to magic me the right key, Costello."

The prisoner smiled back, called him a spoilsport, and gave him the three others he'd slipped from the sleeping guard.

Longarm made sure the impish prisoner hadn't held out on him again. When one of the keys really turned in the lock he nodded in satisfaction, turned, and prodded the unconscious guard as he said, "Rise and shine, Sleeping Beauty. It's a good thing for you I'm not the officer of the day."

The guard didn't wake up, and when Longarm prodded him harder he began to roll off the chair. Longarm caught him in time to keep his skull from cracking on the cement floor. He lowered him to the same, more gently, felt the side of his fat neck to make sure he was still alive, and glanced up ominously at the innocently smiling prisoner to ask, "How did you do it?"

The Great Costello shrugged and asked, "Do I get a stay of execution if I tell you?"

"That's not up to me to say and we both know it."

"We professional magicians never give away the secrets of our craft. You're pretty good, too, considering I don't recall you as a member of our guild. A few more minutes and I might have shown you a *really* neat trick."

Longarm rose to his feet, drew his .44, and fired it down the length of the cell block where the slug wouldn't do too much damage. The Great Costello said, "All right. You've shown the audience your gun is loaded. What happens now?"

Longarm didn't have to answer. For naturally, what happened next was the guards running back from out front, along with the railroad dick. As they all asked questions at once, Longarm shushed them with a wave of his smoking six-gun, and said, "For openers, this gent at my feet has been drugged and may need a doc. How about that, Costello?"

The prisoner shrugged and replied, "I'm an illusionist, not a killer. He'll be all right, once he sleeps it off."

Longarm turned back to the guards that were still functioning. "Carry him out front and see if smelling salts work. I'd still get a doc if I was you."

One of them said, "We ought to have one any minute. They've borrowed an army surgeon to make sure of this other son of a bitch at six, and six won't be soon enough for me!"

The Great Costello grinned out through the bars and told them he wouldn't mind if they wanted to put things off until, hell, a month or more. The railroad dick growled, "Let me in with him. I want to see how sassy he can talk without no teeth."

Longarm put his reloaded gun away as he soothed,

27

"Let him enjoy his fool self, Wagner. Why don't you give these other boys a hand with their heftier pard? I'll hold the fort until we get more help with this ferocious runt."

Wagner bitched about it, but even he could see the unconscious guard was a three-man load. As they toted the drugged man away, Longarm turned the vacated bentwood chair around, straddled it to face the cell door, and told the Great Costello, "I've been anxious to kill time. What other amusements do you have to offer as we await the rooster crow or the hangman, whichever gets here first?"

The prisoner said, "Well, I could show you some swell card tricks, if they hadn't found that last deck of cards I had on me. Is it too much to ask just what you'll be up to as I put on my last performance?"

"I'm here to make sure the final curtain comes down smooth. I have to confess I didn't know, until just now, why they felt they needed extra help with you. How did such a slick cuss like you ever get captured, more than once?"

The Great Costello gripped the bars so he could shove one booted foot through them, saying, "This is no doubt the main reason I tend to stand out in a crowd."

Longarm stared soberly down at the oddly shaped as well as expensive black boot on the man's right foot. It's wearer said, "It's not really a cloven hoof. That was my press agent's idea. But between a natural clubbed foot and my rather elfin Tuath Beag features, I suppose I was a natural for the part of Satan and—"

"Hold on," Longarm cut in. "I understand all but that part about a Twabig. What are we talking about?"

The prisoner grimaced and said, "I didn't think you looked Irish. The Tuath Beag, or Little People, were real. Long before the Celts arrived in the British Isles a smaller, darker race was in residence. Pockets of them still account for rather odd looking villagers in the western counties and, of course, for the old tales of little people lurking about the bogs and under mushrooms. Clan Costello, of course, was Anglo-Norman to begin with. But many a Mayo maiden was pretty as well as small and dark, so . . ."

"I didn't know Costello was an Irish name. I thought it was something more Latin you picked up to use as a stage name. You mean you were really dumb enough to hold up trains under your right name?"

The prisoner sighed. "Had not that guard turned up when he wasn't supposed to, the Denver & Rio Grande would have had to blame the whole affair on the Little People. For it's devil a clue we'd have left them. As for my stage name, I've never been ashamed to bear the proud title of my noble ancestor, Sir Gilbert MacOis-dealbhaigh de Nangle, Baron of Mayo."

"I can see why they might have wanted to shorten that to Costello," Longarm said. "After you went to work as a stage magician you tried robbing silver shipments with a gang, not on your lonesome. Would you like to tell me how some of their names might be pronounced?"

The prisoner shook his head and said, "They offered to spare me from the gallows if I'd inform on my friends. I may look satanic, but I'd die before I'd give you one name."

Longarm heard footsteps in the dark distance and said, "You sure figure to, any time now. Look, no shit, we might still be able to cut a deal, Costello. I know the railroad would ask for a stay if I could tell 'em you was ready to clear up some loose ends for 'em."

The prisoner smiled gamely and said, "I'm supposed to offer dirty deals, not you. Can't you see I'm an imp of the Devil?"

Longarm didn't answer. He got back to his feet as the small crowd of other interested parties joined them. He recognized Father Packer of Fourteen Holy Martyrs and, with less enthusiasm, Topkick Thompson, the local hangman. Thompson was a retired army sergeant who augmented his pension by executing federal prisoners as the need arose. He was a runty old goat with a drinker's nose and rotten teeth. An occasional bath might have helped him smell a mite less disgusting. The others were guards Longarm didn't know or civilians Thompson had likely brought along to help. As the old hangman got within speaking range he called out, "I gotta measure you now sweetheart. We wouldn't want the rope tearing off your pretty little head if we guessed wrong about the drop, would we?"

The kindly Father Packer looked at Longarm and sighed, "Do we have to put the poor sinner through all this, Deputy Long?"

"I fear we do, Father. I don't like Thompson neither, but he knows his job and he's right about the need to do things scientifically."

He took out the key he'd gotten from the Great Costello and opened the cell door. Then he, the priest, and the guards stood aside as Thompson and his crew entered to weigh the prisoner by feel and judge the strength of his neck. It didn't take long. The hangman gave the prisoner a not unfriendly slap on the back and said, "Nine feet and you won't feel a thing, old son. You'll shit your pants and dance like a puppet on a string for a spell, but you won't know it, so what the hell."

Longarm growled, "Cut that out. I mean it."

The hangman came out, looking injured, to say, "Hell, a little humor serves to lighten up the proceedings, Longarm."

The priest went in next. Longarm turned to one of the guards and asked, "Have you boys seen hide or hair of Deputy Guilfoyle? I told him to meet me here."

They looked blank. Then one said, "Oh, you must mean that old boy who keeps running to the crapper. He

30

did say he was from your office. He's out front, if he ain't in the crapper."

Longarm saw they had a handle on the situation in the cell block, so he excused himself to go looking for his errant sidekick.

Out front, he found a very pasty-faced Deputy Guilfoyle seated near a gun rack with Crawford. They both looked sick as hell. When Longarm asked how come, Crawford responded, "We were just talking about that. There must be some bug going around, for neither of us are dumb enough to trust the city water."

"I'm starting to feel better," Guilfoyle said, "now that I've emptied my guts a lot from both ends. I thought I was a gone goose, earlier. Some of the guards called in sick, too. It has to be the water, even though I don't recall the last time I was tempted to drink anything that sissy. I never had supper with old Crawford, and none of the others who've come down with the trots could have eaten with either of us."

Longarm turned, spotted the guard he'd met earlier in the taproom across the way, and asked, "Are you all right? How many others are we talking about?"

The guard, who looked more under the weather from strong drink than illness, said, "We only lost a couple of boys to whatever's going around. I heard about the way old Collins was drugged, but I'm way ahead of you. Their later shift pards are covering for the ones that couldn't make it, and nobody here right now is too sick to hang that rascal out back. I sure wish it was time to start though."

Longarm took out his watch, nodded, and said, "It won't be all that long now. I'd best go back and make sure the Great Costello don't take sick before they can hang him."

Chapter 5

As always, the last few minutes seemed to take forever. Then at last the time arrived, and Longarm got to walk slower than he felt like behind the Great Costello, as the others to either side led him out back.

The sun was up—as Longarm had warned Cynthia Morton it would be—as the execution party crossed the bare dirt yard to the ominously high gallows dominating the scene. Longarm looked for a straw boater perched atop a red head in the considerable crowd assembled to watch. Then he warned himself to keep his eye on the prisoner, for if the Great Costello ever meant to prove he was a great escape artist, his time was about up.

Longarm saw the cuffs were still on the dapper little man's wrists; he had chosen to walk behind Costello with that in mind. Deputy Guilfoyle was backing Longarm's play, to Longarm's left. He still looked green around the gills, but Longarm knew he was a good man as long as he was on his feet. The hangman and his own helpers were well out front and already mounting the

platform by the time the prisoner was halfway there.
The warden and the army doc who'd make sure of the
results were stationed at ground level, to step under the
gallows once Costello hit the end of the rope.

Longarm knew it more usual to have the warden topside, so he could read the death warrant to the condemned man without having to shout, and surmised the
worried warden's reasons for posting himself where he
had. He told Guilfoyle, "You'd best go back the warden
and the doc, just in case Costello tries to escape on the
way down."

Guilfoyle grimaced and said, "He won't." But he
dropped out and headed that way to leave Longarm the
job of watching the prisoner's cuffed wrists.

The Great Costello didn't seem to be trying to slip
either small hand free. Father Packer went up the steep
steps ahead of him, head down as if in prayer, or to
make sure he didn't bust his own neck in the process.
The Great Costello hesitated for a moment at the foot of
the fatal flight, then a guard had him by either arm and
he was going up, gamely or otherwise.

That left it Longarm's turn to mount the gallows. He
was glad he'd get to come back down the same way.
There were fourteen risers. He smiled thinly as that reminded him of the room number Guilfoyle had chosen
as a good place to catch the trots. Longarm wondered if
he'd given them to that gal he'd met or if she'd given
them to him.

Longarm had watched Topkick Thompson work before. That was another reason he didn't like the literally
dirty old man. But there was something to be said for
old Thompson's crude manners. If one had to hang a
man at all, it was likely best to get it over with as sudden as possible. Longarm was still on the steps with the
pine planking of the platform at waist level when he saw
that sure enough they had the black hood over the Great
Costello's head already—Thompson and his boys

weren't paid by the hour. Longarm saw no need to go any higher.

As the warden stepped out into the sunlight between the shadow of death and the expectant crowd, Longarm heard a high pitched voice call his name. He turned to wave back at the distant redhead waving her kerchief at him. He wondered if she'd changed her mind, and if his back would be able to take it.

Then things got confusing as hell for a time.

The warden had no sooner commenced a shouted death sentence when the Great Costello began to throw a temper tantrum. Like a mean little kid who just plain didn't care if it was bedtime, the cuffed and hooded runt dropped to the pine planks and began to kick and thrash. He kicked Father Packer's legs out from under him, and by the time the priest was down, old Topkick and at least two others were the same way. It looked like most of the others were diving on the pile-up of their own accord. Longarm decided he'd only get in the way, or get kicked in the head if he pitched in, so he stayed put as the scene became a chaos of flailing limbs and obscene remarks about someone's mother. Then two guards were rising from the writhing mass with the doomed and hooded wiggle-worm between them; one punched him where his jaw had to be under the black poplin and the other slipped the noose over his head. Then someone else had made it to the trip lever and, whether on purpose or in panic, the trap was sprung and the victim plummeted to his doom with Father Packer and two others to keep him company.

Longarm gasped, "Thunderation!" above the horrified roar of the crowd. Then he drew his .44 and moved most of the way back down by jumping.

As he ducked under the gallows he could see at a glance the execution had indeed taken place, if not as sedately as it might have. Father Packer was sitting up, dusty and confused but not badly hurt. The two men who'd fallen through the trap with him were in about the same dust-spitting condition. Above them, the gent who hadn't made it all the way down twisted slowly at the end of the rope, the piss from one boot tip tracing a dotted circle of mud in the dust below.

Longarm holstered his pistol with a sigh as he stared morosely at the slowly rotating boots. Then he gasped and shouted, "Oh, shit, cut him down!" before he drew his gun again and lit out for parts unknown, cussing fit to bust.

Deputy Guilfoyle shouted the order up through the trap above them. The army surgeon protested, "Wait, we want to be sure."

Guilfoyle insisted, "Cut him down, damn it! Longarm never gives an order just to see if there might be an echo!"

So someone topside cut the rope. The body fell limply to the dust with a sickening thud. As Father Packer crawled over to begin the last rights, the surgeon put his stethoscope to the hanged man's chest and declared, "I pronounce this poor son of a bitch dead and will someone please tell me what's going on?"

Deputy Guilfoyle said he didn't know, either, as he hunkered near the head to haul off the black hood. He'd just gotten it off when someone shouted down through the trap, "Hey, is old Topkick Thompson down there with you boys?"

Guilfoyle ignored the collective gasp from the others around him as he shouted back, "He surely is. I don't know how in thunder you done it, but you boys just hung the hangman!"

Chapter 6

Longarm had of course known they'd hung the wrong man the moment he'd noticed those matching boots. So even before the others had it figured, he'd bulled his way through the crowd to the only gateway leading anywhere but back through the lockup. He told the guards stationed there not to let anyone else out just yet. Beyond the gate lay a lot that usually was vacant, but at the moment was occupied by parked carriages and tethered mounts the crowd had arrived aboard. He ran on, gun in hand, to the side street beyond. The far side was blocked by brick warehousing. To his left the street led back to downtown Denver. To his right the street dead-ended against an eight-foot wall of planking. He headed that way, knowing the railroad yards lay just beyond the fence. He had reason to assume, before he got there, that he was guessing right. A knothole in the barrier blossomed gunsmoke, and a hornet-humming slug whipped past his left ear too close for comfort. He fired his own sidearm into the planking just below the other marksman's smoke signals and kept going, pumping more lead in the general direction he was charging.

By the time he made it to the fence he was hammering dry. So he had to pause and reload before he holstered his .44, took a running jump, and caught the splintery top of the barrier with both hands. He hauled himself up with no trouble, but as he risked a cautious peek over the top someone shot his hat off. So, knowing what came next, Longarm let go and dropped flat in the love grass and sheep shit on his side of the planking. Sure enough, a whole mess of bullets tore hell out of the dry planking his belly might have been pressed to if he hadn't been so smart. There had to be a better way.

As his unseen enemy paused to reload, or run like hell, Longarm rolled back on his boot heels and moved over to where the fencing ended against a brick warehouse wall. As he'd hoped, he found a narrow gap occasioned by the simple fact that boards and bricks didn't come in the same dimensions. By pressing his cheek to the bricks he was able to peer into the Burlington yards. But after that it was all down-grade. He could see acres of empty rail sidings and even some parked boxcars in the dusty distance, but the only thing moving out there now was a tumbleweed, and it wasn't moving enough to matter.

Somewhere a locomotive was releasing steam. He couldn't see it, but it sounded like a switch engine. He muttered, "All right, if we didn't hop a handy freight we're still somewhere in Denver, in shirt sleeves, with a clubfoot and a face that's easy to remember. Said face might appear on some old vaudeville posters, making an all-points even easier."

He heard footsteps behind him and turned to see the senior guard he knew from the night before approaching with his own gun drawn. Longarm put his .44 away with a weary smile and said, "We get to look for him the less amusing way, knocking on doors. He got a good quarter mile lead on me because I just didn't think this was a good day to die. Where he got that .45 is no doubt another trade secret of his occult craft."

The guard said, "The folk back yonder are clamoring to bust loose. Most of 'em seem to be reporters who insist they'll lose their jobs if we don't let 'em print how dumb we just were, in this afternoon's editions, coast to coast."

"That's the trouble with the damned old Constitution. It don't let us hold anyone without due process, and we'd play hell convincing any honest judge someone in that crowd slipped the little bastard a .45 as he was. . . . Hold it. How could he have made it through that crowd and out the gate ahead of me?"

The senior guard put his own gun away as he replied, "Don't ask me. The boys at the gate say you was the only one as left the grounds by that exit."

As they headed back together, Longarm said, "Yeah, the Great Costello is the escape artist he boasted of being. I'm missing something—stage magicians call it misdirection. I know because I've gotten to know more than one magician-gal in the biblical sense. They get you to look one way whilst they're doing something else."

"Well, he surely pulled the hood as well as considerable wool over Topkick Thompson's eyes. How the hell do you reckon he got them cuffs and that hood on his hangman in front of God and everyone else?"

Longarm growled, "I don't know. I never said I was a magician myself, damn it. I can't say what God might have seen, but from where I was standing it was confusing as hell. I can see where old Topkick wound up, some damned way. What's even more confusing is where in thunder the Great Costello went after trading places with him."

They came to where Longarm's hat lay upside down on the cinder paving. He picked it up, dusted it off on his pants, and put it back on as he added thoughtfully, "I can see how the guards could mistake one gent with a hood over his head for another. But that leaves the Great Costello bare-faced in broad-ass daylight for at least a few seconds as they all untangled from one another high above the ground with a whole crowd watching. Then he had to make it out of the prison yard in the same broad-ass daylight, beat me to that fence by a city-block lead with one bum foot and...yeah, he's really one mysterious little gent."

They moved back through the parked carriages and tethered horses to the noisy gate. It was noisy because everyone inside wanted to get out and the guards wouldn't let them out.

The senior guard asked Longarm's views on the matter. Longarm shrugged and said, "I reckon we have to." Then he added, "Wait, tell your boys to let 'em out Indian file and grab anyone with a clubfoot no matter what they look like or who they say they might be."

The guard nodded but asked, "How could he still be inside if you was just swapping shots with him so far off?"

"It works as well another way," Longarm explained. "Costello refused to name the gents who were in on that robbery with him. They just might feel the same loyalty to him, see?"

"Not hardly. Why would a gang member you didn't know want to shoot at you, Longarm? What call would a total stranger have to suspicion you was chasing him?"

"Like I said, they call it misdirection. Stay here and check the boots of everyone on their way out. I have to go in and ask all sorts of dumb questions now."

He did. But the only thing Guilfoyle and the others had down as certainty, even this late, was that Topkick Thompson was dead. None of the late hangman's crew could say whose notion it had been to trip the trap under him. One said, "Topkick liked to do that his ownself. None of us was allowed to even touch the handle. Our

40

job was just to hold the cuss steady as Topkick noosed and positioned him right, see?"

Longarm thought back and turned to the warden as he said, "I recall two of your men hoisting the gent we all mistook for the prisoner to his feet. If it wasn't one of the hanging crew who tripped the trap, that leaves Father Packer and your guards. Since we have good reason to doubt it could have been Father Packer, we'd best have a word with all your boys, Warden."

The warden turned to the nearest uniformed guard in sight and said, "You heard the man, Hansen. Gather all the guards who were even out here in the yard just now. On the double."

As young Hansen lit out to do so, it gave Longarm time for a word with the army surgeon. "I can see why you let 'em carry the dead man inside, Doc. Is it safe for me to assume you can say for certain he died by hanging and hanging alone?"

The army surgeon frowned and asked, "What do you mean? I saw him fall a good nine feet with a rope around his neck and then I saw him stop, with a sickening snap, well clear of the ground. What else do you have in mind as the cause of death, a bad cold?"

Longarm explained, "It would be a lot easier to put handcuffs and a hood on a man who wasn't really struggling. Costello somehow slipped Thompson's frock coat off, as well. Could you say for sure that the old gent was alive and well when he hit the end of that rope?"

The surgeon blinked, nodded soberly, and said, "I meant to do an autopsy in any case. Get in touch with me, say, just before lunch. Now that you mention it, his bladder control could have let go any time between them all going down together and his neck snapping, a few short moments later."

The guard sent to herd all the others together had made it back by now, with only two comrades. He told

41

the warden, "Duffy and Wessel are helping Sergeant Greenwood at the gate, sir. So we're what's left."

The warden frowned and replied, "Where are the others? I detailed an eight-man squad, damn it."

Longarm didn't wait to hear Hansen's answer. He was already elbowing his way through the last of the crowd. Guilfoyle caught up with him near the gate to ask, "Would you let me in on what we're doing now pard?"

"They slickered us with ringers. Do you know why you and Crawford got sick last night? Someone at the hotel spiked your drinks. Did that gal you spent the night with wake up with the trots this morning?"

"Hard to say. She was snoring when you banged on the door. Why?"

"It was just as likely done to you and all the others in that crowded taproom. I don't know about you, but I suspect that harmless newspaper man was poisoned just to establish something was going around. Nobody thought nothing of it when strange faces showed up to fill in for sick guards, saying they was from the other shift."

Guilfoyle snorted in disbelief and protested, "Come on, that would take more balls than seven range bulls could rack up. I can see how a morning-shift man might buy a stranger as an afternoon man. But if even one real guard had showed up, as brave as I did—"

"I know," Longarm cut in. "That's why I'm more concerned about those missing guards than I am about you and Crawford. You two was supposed to survive, as misdirection."

They got to the gate. It was obvious more than half the crowd had left by now and nobody still inside was wearing a federal uniform. Longarm quickly filled in the senior guard on the newest problem and asked, "I don't suppose you boys would have noticed if one of those mysterious extra hands had strolled past you in other duds?"

Sergeant Greenwood said, "Sure we would have. It's going on seven-thirty with the sun up, and none of us are blind. Ain't one gent with a clubfoot passed this way, neither."

Longarm nodded, then he had to ask if there was any other way out. Before Greenwood mentioned it, Longarm groaned and said, "Oh, shit, of course."

Greenwood said, "I reckon anyone in uniform could just walk through the back door and out the front, looking innocent and walking slow."

Longarm turned to Guilfoyle and said, "Check it out," although they both knew it was likely too late by now. As his sidekick lit out for the rear entrance of the lockup, Longarm turned to stare at what was left of the crowd. He didn't see Cynthia Morton or any other gals, although Greenwood said more than one woman with odd tastes in entertainment had left a mite earlier. He saw Crawford about the same time the reporter spotted him and dropped out of line to ask what on earth was up.

Longarm was getting mighty tired of explaining the unexplainable by this time. But he owed Crawford for past favors, and had to feed him at least the basic facts. When he'd finished, Crawford whistled softly and said, "I'm glad I was only slipped a Mickey. For a while there, I thought I was coming down with the cholera. I'll make sure my paper leaves your name off the list of fools, old pard. It's not as if they slickered you, personal."

Longarm growled, "I'm taking it personal. Billy Vail sent me and Guilfoyle to watch out for just what we failed to spot in time. I'll bet that tricky little rascal is laughing his fool head off even as we speak."

"Oh, I don't know, Longarm. If I had you after me, I imagine I'd be up to more running than laughing.

Knowing you, I feel sure you'll cut his trail soon enough."

"I wish I knew me with half that much admiration," Longarm said. "Don't look now, but most of Denver is paved over these days. Cutting sign on stone, road tar, or even cinders can be a bitch. I have no idea where to even start."

Then, as if that had been a theatrical cue, a copper-badge from Denver P.D. pushed through from outside, shouting for U.S. Deputy Long. Longarm waved him over and asked what was up.

The city lawman said, "It's more like three down. Chambermaid at a neighborhood hotel just found three gents in three beds, shot dead in the wee small hours as far as we can tell. Sergeant Nolan said you was good at such matters and so, seeing as you was within easy walking distance . . ."

Longarm started to say he was too busy for a local homicide investigation. Then he counted in his head and said, "Shit, eight men add up to a squad, and we can only account for five who ought to be here." He nudged Greenwood from behind and said, "Come on. I hope I'm wrong, but if I'm not, you'd know your regular shift's faces better than I would."

Chapter 7

As he'd more than hoped it might not be, Longarm saw
the beat man was indeed leading them to the same
damned yellow-brick hotel across the way from the federal lockup. It looked even seedier in the clear morning
light. With the federal guard and Crawford in tow,
Longarm followed the copper-badge to the second floor.
Down the hallway a piece stood Sergeant Nolan,
Denver P.D., in an open doorway. As they joined him,
Longarm noted it was room number 215. Inside, spread-
eagle on a bed, lay a man smiling up at the pressed tin
ceiling with a little blue hole in his forehead. He was
naked, save for his undershirt. Sergeant Greenwood
gasped and said, "Jesus H. Christ, that's Ryan, one of
the boys who called in sick last night!"

Longarm grimaced and said, "What you really mean
is that a total stranger turned up, in his uniform, to tell
you he was sick but not to worry about it, seeing you
had a replacement."

Nolan said, "I'm glad you just explained his missing

duds for us, Longarm. I knew it was a good idea to send for you. We've been wondering how come none of the victims seem to have checked in with any clothes on. The clerk on duty last night don't recall even one of 'em checking in at all."

"Let's have a look at the others," Longarm said.

They did. A guard Greenwood identified as Bill Miller lay dead in bed in 218, while one Isaac Bradshaw had managed to get murdered in 223. None of them looked as if they'd died of the cholera. Each had the same ugly wound in his forehead. When Crawford made a note of that, Nolan held out a palm full of brass and said, "All shot with the same .32 whore pistol. Likely a garter derringer."

Crawford didn't know as much about firearms as most lawmen, so he asked what made Denver P.D. so sure of that. "You don't leave brass on the rug unless you reload," Nolan said. "Such ladylike weapons are usually single shot, so you have to. The shells are not only the same make, but hammer-marked the same way. That adds up to one gun in my book. What do you say, Longarm?"

The younger but sometimes wiser federal man took the brass and examined the hammer marks as he opined, "Well, say all three were fed knock-out drops by their companions. It's possible one killer wandered from room to room with the same gun, but after that it gets mighty murksome. I've never heard even a derringer fire with no noise. Have you, Nolan?"

The burly Denver lawman scowled and said, "Of course not. It ain't possible to fire a gun silent. What of it?"

"That first one, Ryan, would seem to have been shot with a sidekick of mine right next door in Room 214. There's no delicate way of putting it, so I hope the *Post* won't print it, but my pard was not alone in bed. Whether he dozed off a spell or not between times, he

46

woke up easy enough when I rapped on the door with nothing noisier than bare knuckles."

Nolan scowled thoughtfully and tried, "All right, say a gun went off, just as a man was coming and—"

"He'd have noticed," Longarm interrupted. "Even if he's more passionate than I give him credit for, I never come hard enough to miss gunshots, three of 'em, within a quarter-mile of my naked hide. I don't want this in the *Post,* neither, but I was in Room 208, cold sober and wide awake, at the time all three of these gents were gunned, or so you say. Since that ain't too possible, I'd say we're missing something here."

Sergeant Greenwood said, "Say, come to study on it, I would have been in the taproom, directly below us, until just before I had to go on duty with these poor cusses already missing. It was crowded and sort of noisy downstairs, but Longarm's right. There ain't enough noise in a taproom at any time to muffle the sound of nearby gunshots."

Crawford suggested, "Hold on, I recall a science filler we ran a spell back about some gent in New England working on a sort of muffler you can screw on a gun barrel."

Longarm shook his head and said, "I read all about that notion, too. Maybe someday someone will be able to invent a silencer for anything more powerful than an air rifle, but so far they ain't got one to work worth mention."

"Well, say they only half-silenced the muzzle blast and you boys upstairs was really going at it hot and heavy."

"Nope. We're talking about three separate gunshots in three separate rooms at three separate times," Longarm said. "Unless I'm an awful sissy, it's my considered opinion that no man screws that hard, that long, and I hardly think my sidekick and me could have been bouncing as a team."

He moved closer to the last victim, bent over, and wet his forefinger before rubbing it around the hole in the dead man's face. He held his hand up to the light and said, "This one wasn't gunned at close range. I didn't notice powder burns on any of the others, either. It sure is a poser, ain't it?"

"What if they were just shot on their way to work?" Crawford asked. "This part of town is sort of deserted in the wee hours, you know. What if they were just bushwhacked some distance away, brought here, and left as they are now to make it look as if they were gunned here after picking up those gals and. . . . Yeah, it does get complicated, don't it?"

Longarm said, "They'd have been stripped on the street right away, unless those ringers enjoy wearing pissy pants. I don't see why anyone would go to the bother of checking three fancy gals into this hotel if all the gang wanted was a place to hide the bodies a spell. It would have been a lot cheaper just to toss 'em over the fence into the Burlington yards. They wouldn't have been noticed much earlier, given at least some imagination with tumbleweeds and rail-yard trash. So, no, I reckon they was lured up here by them gals, talked into taking off their duds, and then killed."

"Damn it, Longarm, you just now said that wasn't possible," Nolan barked.

Longarm shook his head. "I only said it was impossible to get away with shooting them. We'll let the medical examiner tell us how they died. Anyone can poke a fool hole in a dead man and leave spent brass for the law to find, right?"

48

Chapter 8

It was pushing eleven-thirty A.M. when Longarm
strolled into the Odion Theatre via the stage door off the
alley leading in from Larimer Street. The doorman
knew Longarm of old, so he just nodded and said,
"Third dressing room from the top of the steps, cowboy.
I hope you know we're putting on a matinee performance in less'n an hour?"

Longarm assured the dirty old man he was there on
official business, and moved deeper into the backstage
gloom. It smelled just the way other such places
smelled, a mixture of rosin dust, old rope, raw lumber,
sweat, and theatrical makeup. It brought back pleasant
memories. He'd once ridden herd on the Divine Sarah
and her French troupe, and of course there'd been that
time he'd spent riding with an opera company who's
star had shone on him a spell.

But the show-gal he'd come to the Odion to see
seemed sort of sore at him when she opened her dress-

ing-room door. She hauled him inside, shut the door, and called him a two-timing brute.

He smiled down at the older but still mighty handsome bleached blonde wearing nothing but an open kimono of red silk as he assured her, "Now, Miss Pearl, you know as well as I do that calling either of us a mere *two*-timer would be a mortal insult to our warm natures."

She laughed despite herself and asked, "How long has it been, a year or more?"

"At least that long, and I've missed you horrible. But to tell the truth, I'm here on law business today."

"Good, grab a seat while I put on my makeup for the savages out front. I was afraid you only wanted to screw me, and the show must go on, in less time than we have for nicer tricks."

Longarm put his hat atop an open steamer trunk and straddled one of the two chairs in the small cluttered room. The voluptuous blonde shrugged off her kimono to reveal she wasn't really blonde. She slid the other chair back from her dressing table and sat down, stark but businesslike, to start powdering her face whiter than Longarm really admired. He knew she had to look sort of spooky on stage. She was billed as "Pearl of Wisdom," and had a sort of mind-reading act. He knew better than to ask her how on earth she could tell what was in a gent's pocket seven rows back from the footlights, with only a regular usher helping her. So as she put on her makeup he told her about the Great Costello and all the mean tricks he'd been pulling of late.

The much more attractive practitioner of illusion wrinkled her pert nose at the mention of her rival and said, "Oh, him. I was on the same bill with his act one time, when I was too young to ask for real money. He never made it to the big time. He was just a mechanic with a lot of stooges — way more stooges than a real pro needs."

Longarm said, "I told you last time, in Omaha, how much I admired the way you can slicker so good working alone, Miss Pearl."

She sniffed and said, "It was Sioux City, and I fail to see why a man who knows me better than my gynecologist has to call me a Miss, damn it."

He chuckled and said, "I was just testing you. I'm sure glad you remember me as well as I remember you, Pearl. But, like you said, the show must go on and I'm hot on the trail of the Great Costello. So could we talk about him some more?"

She put down her powder puff and began to paint black eyebrows as she told him, "I can see a dozen ways he could have worked that escape on you. It's easy enough to fool you rubes when we're up on the stage and you're expecting something mysterious to happen. With everyone expecting to see a hanging, not a rabbit out of a hat, an average troupe of stooges under the direction of even a fair illusionist has many an old chestnut to choose from."

Longarm suppressed a yawn and said, "I had that much figured out already. How do you figure they spirited him off the gallows platform in full view of the crowd, once they'd slipped his hood and cuffs on the wrong man and hung him instead?"

She didn't answer until she'd finished painting her already lush lips a size larger, fire-engine red. Then she reached for a horsetail of blonde hair to augment her own natural tresses and commenced to comb it in, saying, "You really must have been half asleep this morning. Didn't you say a couple of men fell through the trap door with the victim?"

"Yeah, one was a priest I know and. . . . Right, in the hangman's frock coat, with dust all over his face and me staring in misdirection at the dead man. . . . I was half asleep. I'd been up all night."

She rose to her feet to face him, hands on hips, to

ask, "How do I look? You look dead on your feet, even sitting down."

He smiled sheepishly up at her painted face and otherwise naked charms and told her, "You look just swell, and I must be in worse shape than I figured. I fail to see how any man who felt the least bit frisky could keep from leaping up at you right now."

She dimpled and said, "Down, boy. I have to get into my corset now, and I know better than to ask for your help, fatigued as you may think you are. Why don't you sleep on the cot behind those drapes over there? I go on in about forty minutes and nobody will bother you back there until I finish my act."

He yawned again but said, "I don't know, Pearl. I'm in hot pursuit of a dangerous and tricky killer."

"Pooh, how are you going to catch even a fly with your eyes half shut? I'm not talking about putting you to bed for the afternoon, you know. But if you'll just be a good boy and lie down for a quick little nap, Mamma might have time to figure out just where you might want to look for that other naughty boy, see?"

He laughed, got to his feet, and said he'd take her up on her kind offer. The cot he found on the far side of the curtains was no doubt long enough for her, but he didn't think it had been intended for anyone as tall as he stood. But she insisted, "Hit the sack before you just fall down, you goof." Then she even helped him into bed, saying, "Now I simply have to get into my costume. Do you want me to close the drapes or do you still like to watch?"

He just laughed weakly and closed his eyes, and just as his head hit her scented pillow, he was out and having awful dreams.

He was stark naked in some spooky woods where the colors were too bright for a moonlit night, like the illustrations in those fairy-tale books. He was walking toward a sort of bonfire. Someone must have thrown salt on the logs, because they were burning green. He didn't know why he wanted to walk closer, even though the naked ladies dancing about the fire were sort of pretty. The Great Costello was standing on the far side, only his face was red as Pearl's lips and he'd sprouted horns. Longarm said, "Howdy, you sneaky cuss. How come you had to kill them other gents if all you wanted to do was escape? No offense, but for a famous escape artist, I didn't find that all that artistic."

The Great Costello laughed and said, "That was what we call misdirection, and now we're going to kill you and make Billy Vail feel misdirected, too."

"I sure wish you wouldn't. I'm late at the office this morning as it is."

The Great Costello said, "Fool, can't you see it's midnight, and Midsummer's Night to boot? Your office isn't open at this hour and, anyway, I mean to sacrifice you to the Devil."

"Oh, I thought you was him. Who are all these naked ladies, pard?" So the Great Costello told him they were imps of the Devil and Longarm said, "Well, I never. I always pictured imps as runty little shits like you."

Then the Great Costello said, "Seize him!" and they all did. He knew he ought to be fighting back harder, but it felt so good to have all those impish gals wriggling against him, and one must not have meant him much harm, as gently as she was jerking him off. So he just kissed her spooky green tit like a sport and then she was saying, "Let's get you undressed, first." He said he was undressed, damn it, and she called him a fool and then he was awake. But the dream was still shaping up to be a wet one as he realized old Pearl of Wisdom was aboard the cot with him, naked as a jay again, with even her face paint wiped away.

"Howdy. Why don't you let go of my tool and let me get outta these duds and in you right," Longarm suggested.

She did. By the time his naked body was pounding hers to glory he was wide awake. She was moving her own lush hips pretty good as well, even as she warned him, "Be careful, God knows where we'll wind up if we crash through his cot. It wasn't purchased with this much activity in mind."

He was willing to slow down. Or at least he was until Pearl moaned, "Oh, hell, forget what I just said, and I promise to forgive you if you break my spine, darling!"

He didn't, even though she seemed pleased by his sincere effort. As they went limp in one another's arms after a long sweet mutual climax, Pearl sighed and said, "That was lovely. But you weigh a ton, and this damned canvas has no springs or padding for a poor girl's frail bones. Let me up. I promise I won't run away if what I still seem to be feeling is all for me."

He laughed and they changed positions. She'd been right about how firm the cot was. As Longarm was trying to get comfortable, she pressed her smaller, softer body down against his firmly enough to keep him deep inside her, even at half mast.

She appeared to have tired herself with all those earlier gyrations as well. For she lay still atop him, nibbling his collar bone with her soft lips a spell before she murmured, "Oh, yum yum yum. Would you mind if we just sort of cuddled like this a while, Custis?"

He ran his hands over her bare spine and behind as he chuckled and said, "I'm not sure Queen Victoria would call this cuddling if she walked in on us just now, but it sure feels friendly. You know, I was having a hell of a dream when you woke me up so nice. I'm pleased as punch to see you ain't really green and wicked looking."

Pearl started teasing with her internal muscles just enough to keep their mutual interest about where it was as she laughed and replied, "I've heard of men wanting to change their luck, but *green* sounds just disgusting.

Why would any man want to screw a green girl, Custis?"

"They weren't exactly gals," he said. "They was imps of Satan."

She made him tell her all about his dream. When he had she said, "I'm glad I woke you up before they had their wicked way with you, dear. But you may be smarter than you think when you dream. As a mentalist, I have to pay attention to the way human heads work. It's not true that dreams foretell the future, but they often tell us things that have been banging about way back in our brains. Who told you that the Great Costello used a lot of female stooges in his old vaudeville act?"

Longarm frowned up at her and said, "Nobody, unless I caught his act one time and forgot all about it."

"There you go. You told me the last time we, uh, cuddled like this, that you came west after the war and knocked around a lot of cowtowns and mining camps before you got a steady job with the Justice Department a few years ago."

"Six or eight years ago. So what?"

"It fits. I told you Costello never made the big time. Six or eight years ago he'd have just been getting started, playing rinky-dink tent shows and so-called opera houses in places like Dodge or smaller, see?"

It wasn't easy to think back in such pleasant present surroundings. He said, "Hold on a minute. I remember seeing many a road show in many a cowtown, drunk or sober, and some of 'em should have been raided. I remember comical acts and trained critter acts the best. To tell the truth, though, I have a tough time paying attention to most magic acts. I can figure out at least a third of the tricks, and don't much care about the others unless they're real gully-washing miracles. I don't mean you ain't interesting, on stage or off. You're sort of astounding in every way. But, I dunno, most stage magicians take forever to get to the trick and then let you down with a fool silk handkerchief or dumpy gal popping out of a box."

"Costello put on an unusually elaborate show with lots of flashing leg and flowing silk. You're right about him building up to pretty basic tricks that most of us could perform without so many stooges. See, it's not smart to build a bigger act than you really need, even in the big time, 'cause you have to split with too many people if and when you get paid. Most vaudeville acts consist of maybe two partners and their in-laws at most."

"Well, he's Irish and the Irish go in for big families," he said. "How would I go about checking on the others he has with him, Pearl?"

"His booking agent might know. You can't trust the names on the three-sheets."

He started to ask what she meant. Then he recalled that the Divine Sarah had posted three lithographed come-ons out front, one to each side of the entrance and one closer to the box office. "You can't trust the hand-drawed pictures on them three-sheets, neither. What's a booking agent, the gent that sets up shows for you folk?"

"Yes. Most of the western circuits are booked out of Chicago. I can ask my own, by wire, if he knows who's been booking the Great Costello and Company. It has to be a small-timer. Do you feel you can be true to me until we get some answers, dear?"

She had him fully erect now, so he told her, and meant it for the moment, that there wasn't a gal in Denver who could pleasure a man half as good as she could. But of course, once they'd about ruined her cot and he had to leave he recalled, with some chagrin, that the Arvada Orphan Asylum would be throwing a fund-raising dance that weekend, and that Miss Morgana Floyd, the head matron, screwed like a mink and was younger and prettier than old Pearl as well.

But there was no way a man who packed a badge could put pleasure before duty, so he was stuck with this mind-reading sex maniac for now whether he wanted to be or not.

Chapter 9

When Longarm joined Billy Vail in his oak-paneled office at the Denver Federal Building, the older and fatter lawman cast a weary glance at the banjo clock on the wall and said, "It's mighty considerate of you to report for work so early, old son. School's out for the summer, but if this was a school day, the kiddies would be getting home about now."

Longarm took a seat in the leather chair across the desk from Vail and reached for a smoke as he said, "Even you must have heard what happened at the hanging this morning, right?"

Vail growled, "I heard about it as I was opening this office no later than six-thirty or seven. The sound of gunplay carries on a clear cool morning. Henry, out front, typed up Guilfoyle's full report, in triplicate, hours ago. I sent him home early because he's got the trots and couldn't tell me where the hell you were, let alone the Great Costello. I'm still waiting."

"Guilfoyle must have told you how we split up. I

wasn't able to follow heel marks across road tar or railroad ballast neither. Did he tell you about them three dead guards at the hotel across from the lockup?"

"No. Denver P.D. did, hours ago. You was wrong about them bullet holes. The medical examiner dug a .32 slug from each victim's brain. It looks like all three were murdered with the same gun by the same cuss."

"Or the same woman, you mean."

Vail shook his head and said, "Either way, it ain't our case. I went over all the reports carefully. Wonder of wonders, I can't see where either you or Guilfoyle fucked up. You got there on time and delivered the condemned man, handcuffed, to his lawsome executioners."

"Then he slipped said cuffs and somehow exchanged places with his hangman," Longarm objected.

"Don't pick nits. The point is that this office done exactly what it was called upon to do. We didn't lose the prisoner, they did. Have you got the trots, too? You look sort of sick, old son."

Longarm shook his head and said, "I'm just tired from questioning so many leads. I've been to every transient hotel in town, and if there's a livery man or railroad clerk in town I missed, shame on me. The gang must have scattered once they busted the Great Costello loose. Nobody recalls hiring a room, a mount, or a railroad seat to more than two or three folk in a bunch. We know Costello's confederates came male and female. Any two could no doubt pass for an innocent couple as long as they didn't act suspicious and—"

"I said it wasn't our case," Vail cut in. In a no-nonsense tone, he went on. "We're off the hook. I mean to keep it that way. The warden at the Federal House of Detention can explain the botched execution any way he wants to. Denver P.D. can solve as many murders in their jurisdiction as they can."

Longarm lit his cheroot and blew smoke out his nostrils as he protested, "Damn it, Billy, counting Topkick Thompson as a human being, the sons-of-bitches have run up a score of five whole federal employees!"

Vail said, "I make it four. Oh, yeah, that guard up near Leadville does make her five. But that case was solved, Longarm. We got the goods on Costello and they convicted him of that killing, just down the hall."

"Ain't busting out of a federal lockup a federal crime?"

Vail beamed across the blotter at him and said, "It is. So's desertion from the army. In either case, the army police or prison administration get to chase the son of a bitch. Unless some other son of a bitch of a judge issues me an arrest warrant on Costello and Company, I don't have to worry about it. I don't want to worry about it. So for Christ's sake pull in your horns and let sleeping dogs snore."

Longarm gripped the cheroot between his teeth too tightly for any smoke to get through as he growled, "Damn it, Billy, they made a thundering fool of me and I've already got a lead or so simmering on the stove."

Vail shook his head and said, "I don't care about your personal likes and dislikes. Have I ever ordered you to stay away from that Sherman Avenue widow woman my wife meets every sabbath at the same damn church? I ain't exactly fond of the Great Costello, neither, but I got an office to run with too heavy a case load and not enough help. No matter how dumb you and Guilfoyle might feel, nobody can point a finger at either of you and say you done one thing wrong. So don't do anything that could leave you looking dumb. That's a direct order."

Longarm could see he meant it. So that was that for the time being and might have been the end of it if the Great Costello had been content with simply vanishing forever.

● ● ●

Orders or no orders, Longarm had made a deal with Pearl of Wisdom and, seeing she'd gone to so much trouble to get the name of a certain Chicago booking agent, Longarm wrote a letter on his own time. By the time Pearl of Wisdom had to leave town, walking sort of stiff, Longarm was able to establish that the Great Costello had indeed been using what amounted to a Celtic clan for his elaborate magic act. The booking agent wrote that while he couldn't give exact names or dates of birth, Costello had last performed along a so-so theatrical circuit accompanied by five young gents and six young gals. Nobody knew which of the gals Costello slept with, assuming he was content with just one. The oversized act had been dropped three years back by the helpful booking agent, and even the small-time circuit, because of their reputation for causing trouble with the other performers. Nobody had ever charged the Great Costello with being anything more than sort of spooky, but the wild kids he used in his act seemed to go in for an unseemly amount of fighting, fornication and, it was hinted, petty theft. The best way to get into a backstage fight with one or more of the clan at once was to even hint at sticky fingers or dressing-room orgies. The booking agent closed by suggesting the act could have shrunk some or grown some since the Great Costello had been forced to book himself as best he could in out-of-the-way show places.

Longarm never showed the information to his boss —Billy Vail was surly enough when he thought you were following his orders. Longarm still drank with Sergeant Nolan whenever their paths crossed at the Parthenon Saloon near the federal building, so he was able to keep up with the investigation of those mysteriously silent hotel murders. But after a time Nolan's boss decided that, what the hell, it was up to the feds to worry about dead federal guards if it was all that big a

62

deal. Longarm had managed to almost forget the gnawing annoyance himself by the time, nearly six weeks later, the damn-fool Great Costello acted up again.

It was payday, the one day of the month Longarm really did his best to get to work on time, and hence the one day of the month Billy Vail didn't get to fuss at him, as a rule. But as Longarm walked into the inner sanctum, putting his wallet away with a less desperate if not entirely satisfied expression on his own tanned face, he saw Billy Vail's pudgy features were beet red and that he was doing a sort of Cheyenne war dance behind his desk. Longarm ducked the ink well Vail threw at him and said, "I give up. You don't look young enough to be having a litter, no offense, and I've been too broke to take your wife out. So what's left?"

Vail threw a balled-up wad of yellow telegraph papers at his senior deputy and wailed, "Read 'em and weep. Then go do something about it, damn it to hell!"

Longarm bent over to pick up the yellow ball before he sat down in the usual leather chair. It took some time to unwad it and flatten the wires enough to read. By the time he was finished Vail had managed to resume his own seat on the far side of the desk, growling, "Wipe that silly grin off your infernal face. What's so goddamned funny about a gut-shot post office clerk in El Paso?"

Longarm said, "It says here that the Texas Rangers don't want the case as a gift, seeing as a federal escapee seems to have cleaned out a federal post office and murdered yet another federal employee in the process. I'll allow footprints coming and going, left by a club-footed suspect wearing a special boot, could lead one to assume the Great Costello needed money some more. But if it was him, he sure has a lot to learn about magic, stage or criminal."

Vail growled, "You read too fast. As I read it, it has

to have been him. The job was planned slicker than most. They even had a fight staged out front to make sure nobody was watching the back, just after that post office closed for the day. The only thing that went wrong was that one postal clerk was working late on the books, after hours. They couldn't have expected him to be there any more than he could have planned on them opening the back door with a lock-pick."

Longarm nodded and said, "It was dumb of that clerk to go for a gun in a drawer, but even dumber for them to kill him so half-ass that he was able to give a description before he died. You'd think a professional magician would know better than to leave distinctive footprints out back, as well. Another magical pal I know says Costello was more flash and dazzle than skill."

"Never mind how you'd have done it, damn it. Thanks to that gunplay, they had to open the safe and make tracks without taking the time to cover 'em. By now it's a safe bet they're spending the money in Juarez. Anyway, the Postmaster General has fond memories of you in connection with other such cases, and the purple-pissing bastard went over my head to ask for you by name. So I have to send you down there. Poke about some, make sure the sneaky little bastard ain't lurking in the United States no more, and then you can come on home."

Longarm frowned and said, "Billy, I share your view that the Great Costello would have club-footed it across the nearby border *poco tiempo*, assuming he has the brains of a gnat. I also know your views on me entering Mexico without an invite from that son of a bitch *El Presidente* Diaz. So can't you see it would be sending me on a fool's errand if I'm not allowed to chase the rascals south of the border?"

"Don't you dare. President Hayes has been cutting the military budget to the bone, so we ain't in shape for another war with Mexico. I know it's a waste of time—

I tried to tell Washington that—but fools will send grown men on fools' errands. So just run down to El Paso long enough to make it look like we tried. Nobody expects you to catch the sons-of-bitches, now that they're long gone."

Longarm rose to his feet with a sigh and said, "I'm on my way. Don't bet on me coming back empty handed. I may have more than one bad habit, but that ain't one of 'em."

Chapter 10

The train ride south to El Paso was uncomfortable and tedious. When the infernal gal he'd been buying soda pop for all afternoon got off at Trinidad, cuss her thirsty hide, he consoled himself with the thought that his Pullman berth was too hot and gritty for decent lovemaking and that she'd have likely burped all night at him anyway.

It was even hotter by the time he and the morning sun had made it to El Paso. The border town stood almost as high above sea level as Denver, and both seemed to be suffering from the same late summer heat wave. El Paso was smaller than Denver if one counted city size by population, but the buildings were more spread out, and most of the streets were still paved with mighty dusty dirt. After he checked into Hotel International and hung his heavy frock coat and shoe-string tie in the closet, Longarm hired a cab for himself and his McClellan saddle. He told the Mex driver to put up the damned top and drive him out to the army remount station at nearby Fort Bliss.

It didn't take long, and for once he got no argument when he showed his credentials to the remount officer and explained his reasons for needing to borrow a government mount for government business. They even let him pick the one he wanted—a chestnut gelding with a black mane and white blaze—and, even better, the critter didn't try to throw him when he saddled and mounted it. So he waved *adios* and headed back the way he'd just come. It felt good to be aboard a decent mount in his shirt sleeves and vest, and to hell with the picky dress regulations of old Rutherford Hayes and his first lady, Lemonade Lucy. The Texas Rangers didn't have to dress sissy, even when their boss was watching.

A lizard darted across the wagon-trace ahead, and though Longarm braced himself for it, the chestnut didn't shy. He patted its neck with his free hand and said, "We're getting along fine, so far. I sure hope your placid nature don't indicate a lack of enthusiasm if we have to go someplace sudden."

He tried a quarter-mile lope to see about that. The army mount didn't argue, and even led with its off forehoof, the way it was supposed to. He reined it to a walk, saying, "I don't know how it happened, but for once the yellow-legs issued me a decent pony to ride. I could tell you tales, old son."

He didn't, of course—a man sounded foolish holding long conversations with a critter. But Longarm was thinking back to another time and another good mount, the chosen favorite of an army officer's spoiled wife who, in the end, had offered a fine ride herself, as he recalled. Her name had been Cynthia, but she'd asked him to call her Sin. He frowned and said, half aloud, "Now that's odd I just now remembered that. The redhead in Denver makes it two sinful Cynthias I could count coup on if I was a kiss-and-teller. But what the hell, I've lost count of the Pats and Billies. I wonder if there's something about naming a girl-child Pat or Billie that predisposes her to grow up sort of passionate."

He decided it was just as likely a man met more Pats and Billies than say Cynthias or Victorias. It seemed natural enough that a gal snippy enough to insist on being called Patricia might not be as good a sport as a good old Pat, and he decided to let the Billies worry about themselves until he met another one. He figured he wouldn't even be thinking about any infernal females this early in the day if that damned brunette hadn't in-sisted on getting off at Trinidad last night. He'd been sent down here to chase owlhoots, not women, he told himself, so he rode the rest of the way back to town in a more serious mood.

The post office that had been robbed was near the railroad depot and not too far from the ford across the Rio Bravo, as the Mexicans insisted on calling it. Since it was their north border, he figured they had the right.

He dismounted, tethered his mount in such shade as there was out front, and went in to see what they had to say about all the money they seemed to be missing.

A pretty ash-blonde secretary gal who looked spunky enough to put up a good fight or a great lay, depending on how she felt about a gent, led Longarm to the back office. An ugly old man waved Longarm to a bentwood chair between his desk and their big old Mosler safe, painted mailbox-green, and said that while he'd be only too proud to help, he didn't really know beans about the case. He added, "I was at home, having dessert, when word came that we'd been robbed. By the time I got here, poor Bob McArdle had breathed his last. They found him on the floor, just about where you're sitting. Seems he'd been sitting in your chair, going over some figures from your side of this desk, when they popped in on him."

Longarm said, "There was something in the report I

read about your assistant going for a gun in a desk drawer?"

The branch manager nodded, slid open a drawer on his side, and produced a big Walker-Colt conversion. He placed it on the green blotter between them and said, "This is it. Naturally, he never got to it. They must have sensed his intent and—"

"It was cold-blooded or trigger-happy," Longarm cut in. "Your man was gut-shot, not back-shot. They might have got him on the rise, but it's more likely they just told him to stand still while they worked on the safe. Then, as they was leaving, one of 'em gunned him. I'll ask 'em when I catch 'em whether McArdle was a hero or whether they just figured dead men tell no tales."

The branch manager gulped and said, "You paint a grim picture either way. But Bob didn't die right away and—"

"You're lucky he didn't," Longarm interrupted. "A while back I worked on another post office robbery, up near Long's Peak, where the owlhoots failed to open a somewhat smaller edition of that same good brand of safe. In that case, the missing money had been pocketed by a crooked postmistress, after they'd given up and lit out."

The older man blanched and gasped, "See here, are you accusing me or one of our employees?"

"Nope. Your dying assistant had no call to lie and he was able to say, or at least gasp, that the ones as shot him opened the safe and took out the money. How much money are we talking, by the way?"

The branch manager looked relieved and said, "Twenty thousand in cash and about five hundred dollars worth of stamps."

Longarm grimaced and said, "The Great Costello must like to write lots of letters. Is there an easy way to cash sheets of stamps without nobody noticing?"

The older man shrugged and said, "A sheet at a time,

maybe. You're as good as they said you were. I'd have never thought of that angle."

"You likely know more than me about running a post office, when it ain't getting robbed. The trick is not to jump to conclusions. The report I read concluded that the gang surprised a man working late, after hours, and gunned him so's they could open the safe; that don't work. The same report says that the town law was just up the street, breaking up a fight, when they heard one gunshot, came running, and found Mister McArdle dying on this floor with the back door open."

"So?"

"So how in thunder would you open a safe, clean it out, and clear the premises that sudden, even if you knew the combination?"

The branch manager tried, "Well, they do say the prime suspect is a professional magician, you know."

Longarm shook his head and said, "Try her this way. They knew McArdle was working alone here, late, after a busy payday week with lots of money orders coming and going. It would have been dumb to rob a post office any other time. While some of the crew staged that street brawl to misdirect any passersby, the others never had to pick no lock. They just knocked on the back door, and when McArdle opened it to see who it was, they pushed in on him, held him at gunpoint, and forced him to give them the combination of that safe."

The dead man's boss protested, "But Bob said they shot him as he was trying to protect the money from them."

Longarm smiled thinly and said, "Dying men have pride, too. He wouldn't have noticed all that much, lying gut-shot on the floor. He said he'd seen them clean out the safe because he had, standing somewhere between where we sit, now, hoping like hell they might let him live. He was no doubt feeling sort of ashamed of himself even before they shot him. He must have felt dumb and mighty bitter when he found himself shot down like a dog as they was leaving, not busting in. That part about not being able to get to that gun in time was as likely a statement of regret as a statement of fact. I feel somewhat better than he must have, now that I see another magician wasn't fibbing about a rival out of jealousy. The Great Costello and his gang ain't such grand wizards, they're simply a cut above your average crook when it comes to planning."

The branch manager sighed and said, "More murderous, as well. We all thought poor old Bob was killed in a fair fight with them."

"I see no call to change his story, official, seeing it was a dying gasp of apology. I'm paid to sniff at dirty linen, and I see no need to wash it in public when I don't have to, do you?"

The older man stared soberly at him and asked, "Do you mean that? Can we leave it at that, with old Bob dying sort of a hero?"

"We won't be able to hold the Great Costello to the dying man's statement, if he chooses to confess the true story. But he might not—he's never confessed to nothing so far. And they didn't send me down here to vex an honest man's kin any more than I have to, so what the hell."

Chapter 11

Longarm went next to El Paso Police Headquarters. He owed the local law a courtesy call in any case and, for all he knew, they might have noticed something that hadn't been included in the reports he'd read so far.

They had. Their chief of detectives sat Longarm down, offered him a big cigar he declined and a shot of rye he didn't, and said, "We've been anxious to hand the case over to a man of your rep, Longarm. We got us a case load this summer beyond all common sense, with another revolution fixing to bust loose in Mexico, just outside our city limits."

He turned to open a sheet-metal file case as Longarm asked, "Do tell? I didn't know your jurisdiction extended across the river. Every time I try to arrest some rascal down Mexico way the infernal *rurales* seem to want me on the less comfortable side of a firing squad."

The detective growled, "We heard how you busted up the Laredo Loop and some *rurales* as well. We don't have to ride south of the border to fight Mexican bandits. The durned old Mexican army and rural police keep chasing 'em up here in droves. You ever hear of a bandit leader called El Gato?"

Longarm looked down at his drink and muttered, "Yep. He says he's a rebel, not a bandit."

The El Paso lawman turned around with what looked like a couple of raw flapjacks in his hands as he said, "Whatever El Gato may be in Mexico, he's considered a bandit by our State Department. I don't know why Washington can't see what a dedicated baby-butchering bastard *El Presidente* Diaz is, but for some reason they can't. So we have orders to arrest El Gato and turn him over to the Mexican authorities whenever he shows his fool face in El Paso and, since he has at least three girlfriends in the Mexican Quarter, he shows his fool face a lot."

He placed the two dirty white slabs of dried plaster on the desk between them and continued, "El Gato's our problem. You can have this as a gift free and simple if it's any use to you."

Longarm could see now that someone smart had made casts of two footprints. One was that of a small but normal looking high-heeled boot. The other looked as if it had been made with a kid's toy flatiron. Longarm nodded and said, "That's my boy. You'd think a gent who fancies himself a master magician would have thought to drag some sacking behind his fool self as he was on his way along a back alley, even in a hurry."

The detective said, "They did. But we got lucky. El Paso had a rare but welcome summer shower the day before the robbery. So while the 'dobe clay behind that post office is usually hard as a brick, it was only crusted dry on the surface and still damp enough under the dust to record the passage of a really heavy bedbug. Like I said, we read signs and found the tied-together tumbleweeds they drug behind 'em. But you're right, they left in a hurry and by now they're learning to like Mexican cooking. You can buy a mess of hot tamales with the amount of cash they got away with."

Longarm pursed his lips and said, "I'm sort of dubious about 'em being in Mexico, no offense. Their style is to blend in between jobs, not stand out like sore thumbs. Costello got picked up after that Leadville job because he's distinctive enough to be recognized from across the street. We don't have even an educated guess as to what the others look like, or even how many there might be. Tell me about that street brawl they staged to lure a crowd away from the post office the other evening."

The El Paso lawman grimaced and said, "I wasn't there. But the beat men who were describe it as a mostly shouting match between a man and a woman. She was doing most of the hitting, with her purse. He seemed content to cuss her and accuse her of all sorts of perversions with some other man. Some of the names he called her was sort of comical, and most of the crowd was laughing, so—"

"Your copper-badges hesitated to move in," Longarm cut in with a knowing nod. "No lawman with a lick of sense would be about to mix in such a fray unless buckets of blood were splashing. Nine times out of ten the woman refuses to press charges in the end, and many an overzealous hero has been stabbed in the back with a hatpin or worse by the very maiden in distress he thought he was saving."

The detective sighed and answered, "Ain't it the truth. From the advantages of hindsight, it's easy to see why the gent kept calling her his cheating wife. Our beat men concentrated most on keeping the crowd from taking sides as they warned the noisy man and woman they'd have to arrest the winner if anyone wound up in need of a doc. They was still going at it when the sound of gunshots rang out down the street."

Longarm said, "Right. By the time anyone thought to

75

ask about the quarreling couple, they were long gone, too?"

"Well, you gotta understand all this razzle-dazzle took place at sunset, in the tricky light of gloaming. The only break we got was that Costello couldn't see well enough to notice he wasn't covering his tracks as good as he must have thought he was."

Longarm nodded, finished his drink, and got up, leaving the casts as well as the shot glass where they were. He said, "I'd be obliged if you'd hold on to that plaster for me. There's an outside chance the prosecution might need it as evidence, and I might bust that soft plaster as I move about more than that file cabinet."

"Sure. We got plenty of room to spare. Where will you be headed next, Ciudad Juarez?"

"Not hardly," Longarm said. "My office frowns on that almost as much as *El Presidente* Diaz and his murdersome *rurales*. If the Great Costello and his gang haven't lit out entire by rail, I figure they're holed up someplace close, here in El Paso."

"We got men watching the railroad depot. We put out an all-points east, west, north, and even informed the Mexican authorities to watch for an impish little club-footed gent."

"That's what I just said. The Great Costello is the only one who has to stay out of sight entire. He's got more innocent-looking help to talk to landladies, go out for food and drink and so forth. He has to know he came out of hiding too soon after that Leadville job. This time he'll figure just to play tar baby until we all lose interest in scouting for him."

"You still ain't said where you're going from here, Longarm."

"I got to go scout for him until I lose interest, of course. My boss implied I was to go through the motions. So that's what I'd best do."

They shook on it and parted friendly. Longarm

mounted up out front and rode back to his hotel. He figured he'd have to poke about the center of town asking questions on foot. He put the chestnut in the hotel stable and tipped the Mex in charge extra to make sure the pony got a good rub, as well as water, before the oats. The Mex looked insulted and said he hadn't bloated a critter since he'd killed his first burro at the age of seven.

Longarm entered the hotel via the side door leading in from the stable. This put him in the stairwell with no need to pass through the lobby. It didn't matter—like most experienced travelers, Longarm made it his practice to hang on to his room key instead of leaving it at the desk every fool time he went out. Few desk clerks really cared, as it saved them a lot of bother as well. They just weren't allowed to tell a guest that.

He'd hired a corner room and bath on the fourth floor, as high as he could get above the hot dusty street and horseflies, with cross ventilation if ever the wind chose to blow again in this oven of a town. The hotel tried to live up to it's grand name by carpeting even it's stairs with medium-priced plush. That may have been why the sneaks in the fourth-floor hallway didn't hear Longarm sneaking up on them. They were no doubt counting on their lookout in the lobby, as well.

Longarm wasn't really trying to sneak, until his eyes rose above the level of the stairwell to take in such odd goings-on. There were two of them, both dressed more town than country, just outside the door of the room he'd hired down at the far end. The glare from the window behind them outlined them too black for him to make out just what they were up to. One was standing with a bulky something in his hand. The other knelt on one knee, trying to pick the lock Longarm never would have locked if he'd wanted strangers messing with his possibles.

Longarm grinned wolfishly, drew his .44, and eased

on up as close as he could get before the one standing with his back to the window spotted him and gasped, "Oh, Christ!"

"That ain't my name, but reach for heaven anyway," Longarm said as he covered both as best he could with one muzzle.

The one kneeling low did no such thing, and as he reached under his coat Longarm fired and put a bullet in one ear and out the other.

Then, as the other made an odd motion with the whatever in his right hand, Longarm shot him dead center and sent him staggering backwards, dropping the object he'd been holding. It thudded hard on the carpeted floor, but he made a lot more noise crashing through the window, landing on the tile roof of the next-door stable, and rolling down and off to wind up in the back alley surrounded by busted tiles and horse apples.

Longarm moved in, saw at a glance that the one still with him was dead as a man could get, with his brains blown out one ear, and it only took a moment later to peer out the shattered window and make sure the other one wasn't going anywhere.

That gave Longarm time to bend over and pick up the odd thing they'd been stealing, or delivering. It was a brass and mahogany Bell telephone. Longarm frowned and muttered, "Oh, shit, if we just shot up a telephone company crew we could be in one hell of a fix!"

Then he remembered there was a telephone just like this one next to the brass bedstead inside, which he hadn't tried to use since he'd checked in. The newfangled Bell telephone was only handy when you knew someone else who had one, and he hardly knew anyone in town. He holstered his six-gun and used his free hand to unlock his door and enter his hired room. He saw at a glance that, sure enough, a twin to the modern wonder he was holding was still where he'd last left it. He closed the door behind him and strode over to pick up the handset and ask, self-consciously, "Howdy. Anybody there?"

He heard some funny buzzing, then a female or just sort of tinny voice replied, "Room service."

Longarm said, "I don't need no rooms served. Is there any way I can call the law on this contraption?"

The gal downstairs replied, "I'm afraid not, sir. We have no lines outside the building, yet. But if you're concerned about gunshots you may have just heard, we've already sent for the police and they should be here any minute."

Longarm said that was good enough and hung up. Then he tossed his hat on the bed, sat down beside it, and studied the extra telephone he'd been somehow blessed with.

The one he had worked good enough, so why had someone been trying to leave him its twin? He got out his pocket knife, opened the screwdriver blade, and got to work on what seemed to be holding the contraption together.

He'd read enough to know more or less how Professor Bell's invention worked. It wasn't supposed to work the way some sly dog had rewired the innards of this one. He heard noise outside and put the invention Professor Bell had never invented gingerly aside as he got back up, went to the door, and opened it, telling the posse assembled, "I can not tell a lie. It was me as shot the sons-of-bitches and they had it coming."

Then he recognized the same detective he'd just talked to at Police Headquarters and added, "Come on in and I'll show you what a swell present they meant to leave for me."

The El Paso lawman and two beat men followed Longarm into his room warily. He picked up the rewired telephone and told them, "Don't worry. I cut the wires attached to the dry cell as soon as I noticed it."

The detectives took the mahogany box-stand to peep into its exposed innards. Then he whistled and said, "Jesus, six quarter-sticks of sixty percent dynamite would be bad enough, but I see they stuck a mess of nails in 'em as well!"

Longarm said, "I don't think they liked me. The plan was to switch this infernal device with my regular set whilst I was out, and it's sure lucky I came home early to change this wilted shirt. If I hadn't, they'd have waited until I came back this evening. Then one of 'em would simply have gone to the desk, asked the operator to ring my room, and blooey. The bell mechanism was set to close the circuit and detonate the bomb, right next to the head of my bed. Even if I'd lived through it, I'd have been off the case for a good spell. My department retires deputies who go deaf in the line of duty."

The El Paso lawman handed the sneaky device back, saying, "All right, we don't get to arrest you after all. Them gents you just gunned down in self-defense may have some I.D. on 'em, and there's even an outside chance it won't be fake. Who do you figure they might have been?"

Longarm put the rigged telephone down beside its innocent twin as he opined, "There's not that much figuring involved. The Great Costello just lost two stooges from his act."

The older and perhaps more cynical lawman said, "Hold on. You could be jumping to conclusions, Longarm. A man with your rep makes enemies, and by now it's no secret you're in town."

Longarm shook his head and insisted, "Men in our line of work make lots of enemies. I've had so many try to shoot me in the back that my shoulder blades itch even when nobody's aiming at 'em. But I can't see the whole James-Younger gang coming with anything this clever if they studied on it all together, sober. On the other hand, at the moment I'm on the trail of a professional magician who goes in for doing sneaksome things with mirrors, trick boxes and such. So add it up."

The detective did, and decided, "Well, this time his stage magic surely backfired on him. Instead of them getting you, you got two of them."

"It turned out worse than that, from their point of view. It tells us for certain that I guessed right about them being holed up near the scene of their last crime," Longarm said. "The Great Costello and likely most of the others are eastern city-bred rascals, but they likely know how to ride. And we know at least one of 'em can shoot, more than common sense might call for. But after that, they can't feel too comfortable in our wide-open western spaces. They feel safer hiding in the cracks of fair-sized towns, like cockroaches."

The detective said, "Well, seeing as they must be somewhere in or about our fair city, I'd say that makes your job a lot easier, right?"

"You must not have ridden with my old outfit in the war. If you had, you'd have had to help us take some towns. So let me tell you, pard, there ain't no more desperate fighting than house to house, even when you're allowed to shoot innocent bystanders. I suspect the Great Costello ain't as worried about that as I have to be, the trigger-happy little bastard."

Chapter 12

After a while, they'd carried the bodies off to the El Paso morgue. The hotel manager had put a hall porter to work on the blood stains and busted glass, asked Longarm to check out, and been told to go to hell. Finally Longarm was free to take a quick bath and put on fresh underwear and a dry shirt, but by the time he got to the Western Union office a short walk away, he was starting to wonder if it had been worth the effort. The afternoon sky above the frying-pan streets of El Paso had clouded over an ominous mottled gray, but that only added to the tropical humidity and made his sweaty legs itch ferociously inside his brown tweed pants and cotton longjohns. The longjohns were supposed to sop up the sweat, which was why men who might have to ride a lot on sudden notice wore the otherwise dumb things. He had no undershirt under his hickory shirt and tweed vest. It didn't help much.

He block-printed an up-to-date report with a sweaty pencil on wilted yellow telegram paper, and told the wilted clerk to send it to Billy Vail, night-letter rates. Old Billy fussed at him for not reporting his progress in the field at all, but fussed almost as much and kept wiring dumb suggestions when he knew what was going on. He couldn't really fire Longarm if he got the progress report sometime tomorrow morning, and Longarm didn't want any further orders just now. The ones he'd left Denver with had sounded dumb enough.

But, having done his duty for the moment, Longarm had to admit this fool's errand seemed to be getting sort of interesting after all. The Great Costello was pretty good at misdirecting the western rubes he felt so superior to, but he had a lot to learn about the owlhoot game he'd chosen as a new trade. The jails and prisons of this imperfect world were filled with fools who'd started out thinking they were smarter than the law, not because the law was all that smart, but because of the way it worked.

The contest was never between one crook and one lawman, like a game of chess. It was between one or at most a small band of wise-ass crooks and all the lawmen, everywhere.

Whether they were as interested or not, the local lawmen had made the right routine moves Longarm never could have managed on his own. Country sheriffs and small town copper-badges were on the alert for the easy-to-spot magician, no matter which way he chose to limp on his deformed right hoof. It was one thing to just lower the curtain when a magic act was over, but things didn't work that way in real life, when the audience really wanted to know how you'd hauled that rabbit out of that hat.

There was a city directory at one end of the Western Union counter. Longarm was going through it when the clerk rejoined him to say, "Your office ought to get that night letter around nine tomorrow morning. What are you looking for in that old out-of-date directory, Deputy Long?"

"It must be out-of-date if you have even one theatrical agent in El Paso, for I can't seem to find such a listing."

The clerk said, "If there's any such person here, he's yet to send a wire asking any actors to come down this way. I notice such unusual trade. We get show business folk in here all the time. El Paso ain't no hick town, and we got more than one vaudeville house, along with the opera and lecture hall. But I suspect touring entertainers are sent here from somewhere else, not the other way around. Why don't you ask up to the opera house? It's just up the street a piece."

"I ain't looking for opera singers. It was a wild shot to begin with. If the rascals I'm after was reconsidering life upon the stage I wouldn't be after 'em so much. I might try a couple of vaudeville doormen to see if they might know any real names matching the descriptions of a couple of cusses we got on ice, though. The names they was packing in their wallets didn't show much imagination, considering how Irish they both looked."

"Suit yourself," the clerk said, "but you'll find vaudeville shows hot and stuffy if we don't get a break in this infernal weather. If you want to see a real show, out where the wind can get at you, what about the *Fiesta de Juarez?* They're throwing it this evening, starting just after sundown."

Longarm sighed and said, "I ain't supposed to cross over to Juarez."

The clerk laughed and said, "Not there, here, in the El Paso Mex Quarter. I don't think *El Presidente* Diaz would let 'em hold such a demonstration in Juarez. When they ain't dancing and strumming, our own Spanish-speaking residents like to make speeches in favor of the Juarez revolution they feel Diaz betrayed."

Longarm said he'd study on it, then left. Billy Vail

hadn't sent him all this way to listen to Mexican political speeches, or even to dance with Mexican gals, although that sounded more like it. He started up the walk, and it was a good thing it was covered most of the way by awnings or 'dobe overhangs. For he hadn't gone far before a streak of lightning ripped the belly out of the swollen gray sky and it commenced to rain fire and salt.

Longarm paused in a dry doorway to light a cheroot. He studied the best way to move on without wading knee-deep in swirling brown water, now that the street had decided it wanted to be a river in flood. The walk was already inches awash and he could only move up on the stone doorstep and hope for the best. His damned matches were supposed to be waterproof, but it took three tries before one was willing to flare. He lit his smoke and watched a dead cat and some driftwood bob by. He smoked the cheroot down, tossed it out to see where it might want to go next, and had just about made up his mind that it wouldn't bore him as much to get wet when, as suddenly as it had begun, the rain stopped and the sun came out to beam down at the flooded streets of El Paso.

He could see by the swift muddy current that all that water had to be running somewhere. He lit another smoke and saw that little islands of horse shit and mud were already forming out there. He waited until the street was running more like old Cherry Creek up in Denver, then was able to cross it dry-shod by leaping from sandbar to sandbar. This at least put him on the same side as his hotel. But he'd no sooner made it than it began to rain again, even harder. He watched the street fill up again and muttered, "I wish you'd make up your mind, Thunderbird." Then he headed back to his hotel. There was no sense drowning unless a man had someplace serious to go. He knew such summer storms never lasted long in these parts, so he decided to wait for fairer weather before he wandered anywhere.

This time he entered the Hotel International by way of the front door. The desk clerk called him over. Longarm expected to be told he'd gotten a wire or even better a police report. But the clerk said, "A lady was in here asking for you, Deputy Long. You just missed her."

Longarm said, "She must have been a mermaid. Did she ask you to ring my room?"

The clerk shook his head and replied, "No. She just asked if you were registered here. I told her you were, since you are, and she said she'd try again, later."

"I don't suppose she left a name before she went swimming some more?" asked Longarm.

He wasn't surprised when the clerk said, "No. She only said something about trying later."

"I wish they'd quit trying altogether. What did she look like?"

"Nice. She was wearing a sort of shapeless slicker and a rain hat, but what there was of her to see was mighty pretty. I couldn't see her hair, but I think her eyes were hazel. Does that sound like anyone you know?"

"Not here in El Paso. If she shows up again, send her right on up. Then ring me on the house phone. It's safe to do that now, I hope."

He went on to climb to the top floor, squishing on the plush a mite this time. When he got to his door he saw the match stem he left jammed just below the bottom hinge was still in place. But just the same, once he was inside, he took the back of the bedside telephone off to make sure it hadn't been fooled with in his absence. It hadn't. The one wired to ring louder had been put in the closet for now.

He got rid of his hat and gun rig, sat on the bed, and hauled off his old stovepipe army boots. Then he changed his socks. It was raining now, if anything, harder than ever. So much for the fiesta they'd planned on for that evening. That left him nothing more entertaining to consider than his mysterious female visitor. So he considered her, stretched out atop the bed covers in his shirt sleeves and socks.

It wasn't true he didn't know any white women at all in El Paso. He'd been through before and recalled a couple with some fondness. But the only Texas gal in recent memory who hadn't said she'd never speak to him was old Jessie Starbuck, better known as Lone Star, and El Paso was west of her usual stomping grounds.

If it had been Jessie, and she really came back, the results were likely to be distracting as well as delightful. For while they always seemed to wind up in bed together, sooner or later, the somewhat ferocious Lone Star hardly ever looked him up unless she wanted him to help her hunt somebody down. He didn't mind feeling a mite used and abused, when he had nothing better to do. But he had his own hunting to tend to in El Paso.

He glanced at the raindrops running down his window panes and yawned. Whoever the gal had been, she'd said she might be back. Meanwhile the door was locked, his .44 hung handy on the bedpost, and he had his derringer in his vest pocket if things got really tricky.

Mulling over the little the clerk had told him, Longarm decided the gal in the slicker didn't work so good as a member of the Great Costello's murderous clan. She hadn't asked the clerk to ring the telephone beside his head, so that couldn't have been her reason—they had no way of knowing whether their comrades had been shot before or after switching the duplicate telephones —unless she didn't want him dead. No gal in cahoots with the Great Costello would have missed that opportunity. She'd have considered it worth a try, at least.

The clerk said she'd asked if he was staying here, as if she didn't know. The Great Costello had known he was, and even the room number, so he'd have had no reason to risk a confederate just to find out what he already knew.

Longarm yawned again and told himself, "There you go again. You know the tricky little bastard depends on misdirection, or getting a man to think along natural lines while he pulls something plain logic would never lead one to expect. We got to keep an open mind, old son. Stage magicians hate to perform in front of children because kids, not having been taught to think logical yet, let their innocent little eyes wander instead of looking where they're told to. We'd best just keep staring, innocent and childlike, until we see him stuffing that rabbit in the hat as bold as brass."

He yawned again and closed his eyes, lulled by the patter of the raindrops and the effort of not thinking too grown-up. Old Pearl of Wisdom had told him an amusing story about a famous stage magician who thundergasted the audience with a trick so simple it seemed impossible to get away with. The cuss had these two big flashy German-silver jars on separate stands, say ten feet apart. He'd hold one up to show everyone how empty it was. Then he'd prance across the stage to the other, with the limelight and drum rolls following him, and show everyone the second one was empty, too. Then he'd go back to the other, talking a blue streak about the wisdom of the ages, and proceed to haul yard after yard of brightly colored silk out of the first one until he was knee-deep in swirling silk. Then he'd go over to the second one and do the same until, moving back and forth, he had that flashy silk all over the damned place and the baffled rubes were so puzzled they were almost scared.

The trick, of course, was that while everyone was watching the magician do his stuff, making sure he wasn't cheating, his soberly dressed and quiet assistants were just stuffing the silk into whichever jar he wasn't fooling with, in full view of an audience that simply wasn't paying any attention to 'em.

Sensible folk thought from A to B to C and so on. Everyone had been fooled at that botched hanging simply because it wasn't logical to even consider two uniformed guards hoisting a hooded man to his feet and putting the noose around his neck if he was not the man they'd come to see hanged. Nobody had spotted the Great Costello slipping away through the confused crowd simply because nobody was expecting a man they'd last seen atop the gallows in a hood and shirt sleeves to pass them by in Topkick Thompson's coat and hat.

Longarm dozed off. He didn't really need the extra forty winks, but he felt more alert than he might have when an officious knock on the door across the room woke him up and put him on his feet, .44 in hand.

He moved over, asked who it was, and when his caller said he was the law, opened the door a crack to see that it was sure enough an El Paso copper-badge. So he lowered the muzzle of his gun and let the local lawman in.

The uniformed beat man said, "I just come over from the morgue. Sergeant Purvis ordered me to tell you that we got a line on the gents you shot up here, earlier."

Longarm had just remembered Purvis was the friendly detective he'd jawed with, earlier, when the beat man handed him an envelope and said, "Their yellow sheets are in there. Sergeant Purvis said you'll find his home address as well, in case you need him. He just went home for the day. Told me to bring them papers to you before I began my own tour of duty."

Longarm glanced at the nearest window and said, "I must have been more tired than I suspicioned. When did the rain stop and what time might it be right now?"

The El Paso lawman said, "After six. The sun will be down all the way in an hour or so. The rain let up hours ago, God bless it. Looks like we're in for a nice cool evening after all."

Longarm thanked him and sent him on his way. Then he put on his boots, strapped on his gun rig, and seeing one could breathe again, put his frock coat on over it to look decent at supper.

He ate downstairs in the hotel dining room while he perused the short but disgusting police records of the two boys he'd had to gun.

The late Tommy O'Horan, devil of a lad that he was, was wanted by the constabulary of County Mayo for robbery and rape, British law setting more value on property than personal injury.

The late Martin Pendergast had immigrated from the same Irish county before getting into trouble as a safe-and-loft man back east. It was said he'd reformed and gone into show business once they let him out of Sing Sing Prison.

Longarm chewed his steak and thought, "That would have been the one working on my lock. Costello said he was from an old Mayo clan, and Pearl of Wisdom said big acts tended to be family affairs. Unless they go in for incest as well, and why not, the gals may just be play-pretties they picked up along the way."

He put the records away and ordered apple pie for dessert from the Mex waitress. She was kind of pretty, but not as pretty as she must have felt she was. She told him she got off in a little while, and asked him if he was planning on attending the big fiesta in her part of town.

He said he didn't know they'd still planned on holding it, seeing as they'd just had at least half of Noah's flood. She said, "Oh, it shoud be even nicer, now that the air is so cool and the stars will be coming out so *romantico*. I am called Rosa, by the way."

He said he still wanted that apple pie and that she could call him Custis. So when she came back with his pie she did and asked if he was going to the fiesta.

91

Before he could ask why she added, "Don Julio Valdez will be there for to make a speech about *democracia en Méjico*. So everyone will be there, and the dancing will go on until dawn, or until one dances with the right person, that is."

He said, "Well, seeing as everyone will be there, I just might wander over and see if anyone I'm looking for is there as well."

Chapter 13

Having made up his mind to view the world with child-like innocence, Longarm found the goings-on in the Mexican Quarter less unsettling than a snooty gringo tourist who wasn't used to the smell of cactus candy and corn-husk-cooked tamales might have.

Mex Town was downwind of the fancier parts of El Paso, near the river and thus handy for unofficial visits to and from old Mexico. The sky above was deep purple and the brick-paved plaza, washed clean by the recent rain, was illuminated every color of the rainbow by paper lanterns dangling in strings overhead. The official festivities hadn't started yet, but that hadn't kept anyone away. The crowd was about three-quarters Hispanic and the rest Anglo. Longarm doubted many of the Anglo-Texicans had come to hear political speeches in Spanish. But, like him, anyone with an open mind enjoyed sprightly music, tangy eats, and the dusky charms of lantern-lit *señoritas* who simply refused to wear their fandango skirts as long, or their lacey white blouses as high, as Queen Victoria was said to approve.

Somewhere across the plaza guitars were strumming a fandango, or a flamenco, as they would persist in calling what any Texan could tell you was a fandango. Small stands vending everything from cactus candy to straw *vaqueros* on straw horses that only a gringo might have any use for were set up all around. A bigger platform draped with red, white, and green bunting dominated one end of the plaza in front of the old 'dobe mission. The folding chairs to either side of the speaker's rostrum were still empty. That was likely why nobody was making a speech. The 'dobe walls behind, mud colored by daylight, formed a backdrop of old gold when illuminated by the soft magic light of paper lanterns. The tricky light made folk look sort of mystic as well. A passing *señorita* could go from a mysterious romantic silhouette to a giggling moon-faced *mestiza* with gold teeth, or vice versa, faster than you could keep track of. Longarm figured a shadowy silhouette could see and not be seen too well, so he looked about for a shady nook the lantern light couldn't get at. There were plenty to choose from.

He'd tried cactus candy before—it tasted like watermelon rind boiled a month or more in brown sugar. He bought a big fat tamale cooked in corn husk and served in a cone of newspaper. Then he backed into a big black shadow to nibble on it with his back braced against 'dobe bricks. It tasted good, but he'd already eaten supper. His main reason for buying it was an excuse to keep his face hidden even better behind something, in case he noticed anyone in the crowd he didn't want to howdy.

He didn't think the Great Costello would dare to show his sardonic face in public this soon. On the other hand, the rest of his gang had less to fear. The rogue magician didn't look much over forty. That could make most of the others younger, and young folk with nothing better to do might enjoy soft lights and loud music as much as anyone else.

From there on, he knew, his notion left enough loose ends to worry a man. He knew what the Great Costello looked like. He knew what O'Horan and Pendergast looked like, on ice. What any other member of the gang might look like was up for grabs. If that booking agent had his numbers right, the Great Costello now had but three male and half a dozen she-male followers to work with. Halfway-decent-looking women without an escort were apt to attract attention anywhere; west of the Big Muddy, where such critters were more scarce, they'd attract more than mild attention—they'd leave a trail of gossip.

Longarm told his hot tamale, "If I was saddled with unescorted outlaw gals, and wanted to move on discreet, I'd either recruit 'em some traveling companions or send 'em some distance, alone."

Then he jumped, "Jesus, I'm dumb," and tossed away the rest of the tamale. But as he strode toward the plaza exit closest to the El Paso railroad depot all hell commenced to bust loose.

Longarm ducked between a food stand and a backup wall as women screamed, men yelled, and hooves pounded on the bricks. As one of the riders reached up with his machete to slash at the line holding up a mess of paper lanterns, Longarm recognized his grim gray sombrero and matching charro jacket for what they meant. Since *los rurales* tended to shoot at him a lot, south of the border, he thought it only right to return the favor when the sons-of-bitches rode north of their own jurisdiction. He blew the rascal out of his saddle.

The Mexican lawman's pony ran on—he didn't. He lay screaming like a woman giving birth on the bricks, just because he had a round of .44-40 in his hide, and the paper lanterns he'd brought down with him had set his uniform on fire. Before Longarm could decide

95

whether or not to shoot him some more, two Mexican gents and a fat old Mexican lady proceeded to put the fire out and stomp him to death at the same time.

Meanwhile, more confusion was busting loose over by the old mission. When someone shouted, *"Viva libertad!"* above the gunfire, Longarm could see the fiesta had degenerated into a heated discussion of Mexican politics. Even if he hadn't already had a better place to go, he knew this was no place for an Anglo in any case. He bulled his way through the still mostly puzzled crowd and only had to pistol-whip one gent who called him a dirty gringo and wouldn't get out of the way. Then he was on a dark side street. The city fathers of El Paso saw no need to put street lights in the Mexican Quarter. Longarm started running and only had to round a few corners before he figured he was in the clear if he didn't meet anyone. He holstered his .44 and headed for the center of town around the railroad depot at a more sedate but hurried pace.

He was annoyed at *los rurales*, but not as mystified by their sudden appearance. Don Julio Valdez had simply picked a piss-poor place to hold a rally against the current Mexican dictatorship. The infernal border was only a mad dash away and *El Presidente* Diaz was no doubt mad as hell at Valdez.

Longarm barely bothered to keep abreast of the confusion south of the border. He had enough on his plate in a country where the government was usually on the side of the law. In Mexico these days, it seemed the only difference between a lawman and a bandit was whether they were riding for the party in power or against it.

He'd read how Don Julio, a big *ranchero* and erstwhile army officer under Juarez, had turned against old General Diaz when that officer, in turn, had taken advantage of the death of Juarez to simply seize the presidency and to hell with elections. They seemed to admire

Diaz in Washington, or perhaps on Wall Street. Diaz had set up what they called a stable government. Long-arm knew what a stable was. The stink of horseshit would knock you down if you didn't clean it out now and again. But every time someone like old Valdez proposed a cleanup, old Diaz had him shot.

Chapter 14

By the time Longarm made it to the depot, even the Anglo law had apparently headed for the Mexican Quarter to deal with the border raid. Longarm wished them well, but doubted they'd get to shoot as many *rurales* as he had. Whether they'd located old Valdez or not in that crowd, by now the raiders would be back across the river. *Los rurales* were no damned good as human beings, but they were good cavalry irregulars. Such outfits were paid to hit and run, not to stand and fight.

Longarm eased into the nearly deserted depot to study the waiting room and ticket window across the way in sober shadowy silence for a spell. The only folk who seemed to be waiting for the next train looked more like homeless drunks than members of a theatrical troupe or even a criminal gang. By sort of squinting he could just make out the timetable chalked on a black-board above the ticket window. "Shit," he muttered, as he saw that while the next eastbound would pass through in a little over an hour, a westbound had just pulled out.

He moved out to the open platform. *Por nada*. If anyone had meant to catch that train for Pueblo de Los Angeles they hadn't missed it. He knew that if he'd been anxious to leave El Paso tonight without too many noticing, he'd have likely made a run for that same train during all the commotion in another part of town.

He shrugged and was about to re-enter the depot when, through the grimy glass of the platform door, he spied a couple coming in from the street via the front entrance. The young gent he'd never seen before escorted the gal he had to a seat near the ticket window. As she sat down, Longarm expected her escort to move over to the window and pay for at least her train ride. But he just turned around and was out the front door by the time Longarm came unstuck and opened the back one.

As he bore down on her, Cynthia Morton looked up, smiled, and asked, "Why, Custis, what are you doing here? I hope you're on your way west with me, dear."

He joined her but remained on his feet as he replied, "That train won't be leaving for an hour. How come you're here so early and who was that gent who just brung you?"

She dimpled up at him and said, "Why, I do believe you're jealous. That was Sam Dillon, another reporter from Kansas City. We both work for the *Star*."

"How come you're working for it here in El Paso?" he asked.

"We came here for the same reasons you did, I imagine. I thought you'd be covering that last robbery the Great Costello pulled off. I asked for you, earlier, at your hotel, but alas, they said you'd gone out."

He didn't answer. She said, "I asked again, this evening, when my paper wired me new orders. There's another Chinese riot going on in California. They feel one

100

reporter here in El Paso may be more than enough to cover your efforts to catch the Costello act. But I did want a chance to, uh, interview you before I had to move on. Have you had any luck at all, dear?"

He smiled and told her, "Not much. But you know what they say about being unlucky at either cards or slap-and-tickle, and your train ain't leaving for a good hour."

She fluttered her lashes and said, "Oh, dear, that doesn't give us nearly enough time, and I've already checked out of my room at the Monarch."

"That's all right. I still have a swell room just up the street, at the Hotel International."

She looked away and murmured, "I know. That's why I tried to find you there, earlier, when there might have been more time."

He bent to haul her gently but firmly to her feet, insisting, "Not time enough is better than no time at all, honey. Come on. Lord knows when we'll meet again and we've plenty of time for a quicky."

She didn't resist, but told him he was just awful and added, "I just got all cleaned up for that long train ride and. . . . Oh, hell, what are we waiting for?"

He laughed, put an arm around her waist, herded her out, and got them headed for his hotel before she could change her mind. She said she was too embarrassed to pass through the lobby bold as brass with a man they had to know had checked in single. So he steered her into the stable and, ignoring the bemused look from a groom currying a horse, smuggled her in the side entrance. She protested he was taking her to the moon as he helped her up the stairs. When he unlocked the door she stepped in first, turned to him with both arms held out to him in the dim light, and murmured, "Come and get it, sweetheart."

So he did. Knowing he'd never get a better chance he just whipped the cuffs out from under the tail of his

101

coat, snapped one loop around her right wrist, and sat her on the bed with a quick shove to finish cuffing her to the brass footrail. Then, as she wailed in dismay, he turned away to slam and lock the door, then struck a match to light the lamp close to the other end of the bed.

Cynthia protested, "Custis, I don't go in for any of that Marquis de Sade business, and how am I to get undressed for you with my hand in such an odd position?"

He sighed, tossed his hat aside, but remained standing as he told her, "I know what you go in for and it sure puts me in a bad spot as the arresting officer. But sometimes the law just has to take what it can get."

She gasped in dismay but tried, "You idiot, why would you want to arrest me? Since when is it a federal offense to work for the *Kansas City Star?*"

He reached for a smoke as he told her, "It ain't, but you don't. The only star you've been working for was at best a star on the small-time stage. I could brag on being smart enough to know no one newspaper sends two reporters out on the same story. Or I could brag I noticed you don't seem to be traveling with no luggage in your hurry to leave town so innocent. But the truth is that it's been a good six weeks since last you misdirected me in Denver, pretending to be working for that newspaper. In that much time a lawman worth his salt has time to make a certain number of inquiries, and while Crawford of the *Post* couldn't say one way or the other, the *Kansas City Star* wrote back that they just didn't have any female reporters by any name, let alone a beautiful redhead with Irish eyes."

She gulped and said, "Oh, I can explain that, dear."

"Let me explain it to you. Your job was to fuck up my head with that same magic potion Guilfoyle and the others got sick on. When I left behind that pitcher of beer you'd likely spiked and turned down your kind offer of another drink up in your room, there was nothing left for you to do but fuck, and for that I'll always remember you fondly."

She wiped at her eyes with her free hand and called him an unfeeling brute. That reminded him he hadn't felt her up for concealed weapons yet. He shoved her flat across the bed and proceeded to do so as he continued, "For a reporter gal with easy access to any police blotter you cared to look at, you sure went to a lot of trouble trying to find out from me, personal, what went wrong with the telephone repairs up here, earlier."

She grabbed his wrist with her free hand to guide his down her belly and between the thighs she'd spread for him under her skirt. He said, "I would have got to that, anyway. But it's nice to know you ain't packing a gun or even underdrawers there."

Then the telephone rang and she sobbed and went stiff all over. He said, "No it won't. Lie still whilst I see who it is."

He rolled away from her, picked up the part you were supposed to hold to your head, and said, "Howdy. *Quien es,* or who's that, as the case may be?"

The Great Costello replied, "Longarm? I fear you have me at a certain disadvantage."

Longarm said, "That's true. Were you hoping to blow us both up or did you have something to say to me?"

"If you look in your closet you'll see we got that other set while you were out. That match stem in the door was clever, but such simple tricks were never meant to fool a professional. I've called to talk about my daughter."

"I was wondering who she might be. Where are you calling from, seeing they told me this is a house phone with no lines running to the outside world?"

The Great Costello sighed and said, "You're too dangerous by half. But needless to say, I could make it out

103

of the building in a few seconds, and will, if you hang up."

"I'm still listening. I wouldn't want to leave my prisoner unguarded long enough to run down all them stairs in any case. You may have taught her too many escape artist tricks."

"That's what I wanted to talk to you about, Longarm. Earlier today you killed the only one of my young helpers who was really a killer, and for that I'd thank you if he wasn't a blood relation. It was Tommy O'Horan who wanted to kill you, just as he killed all the others. I couldn't turn the lad away to fend for himself. But he was a loose cannon on the deck indeed and, well, you got him. Now about Maureen . . ."

"I thought her name was Sin," Longarm said. "Spare me the yarns about her purity, old son. Whether she ever killed anyone personal or not, I got her on Murder One and, whilst I admire her pretty neck a heap, she'll have to sing like a mockingbird to save it now. So how's about hanging up so I can call down to room service for someone there to fetch me some backup?"

The Great Costello said, "It's not her you want. It's me. I'm the one who planned the tricks and failed to control Tom O'Horan."

Longarm smiled fondly at the handcuffed redhead at the far end of the bed and said, "That's true. But you and the others are still birds in the bush, so I'll just have to settle for the redbird in my hand, for now."

The Great Costello sighed and asked, "How do you feel about an even trade? Me for my daughter, with an hour's lead for her and the others?"

Longarm knew no train would be leaving within an hour, and that all the trails out of town would be in mighty good shape for tracking until that fresh surface got chewed up by other traffic, but he didn't think he ought to point that out. He said, "That sounds fair. How do you propose we work it?"

"You let her go. As soon as she's in the clear I'll come up to your room and surrender. Deal?"

Longarm snorted in disgust and said, "I'd feel safer buying a gold brick from Soapy Smith. What's to stop you from just running off with her, laughing like a jackass at the lawman foolish enough to even consider that?"

"You have my word as a man of Clan Costello. If you know anything at all about me you know my work is good. It may be true that one has to read the fine print when dealing with us satanic types, but it's against my craftman's code to just plain lie to the audience."

Longarm had reservations about that. He'd heard more than one stage magician say the hat was empty just before he hauled a fool rabbit out of it. On the other hand, he only had a morals charge on the girl for certain, and wasn't looking forward to explaining that part in court if her lawyer brought it up. He knew there was an outside chance the Great Costello's word was worth a fart in a windstorm, and that having caught the redhead once there was always some hope of catching such an easy-to-notice suspect again. So he said, "I ought to have my head examined, but I'll meet you halfway. You come up the stairs as high as you feel is safe. I'll let the girl go and watch from my doorway. As she drops down the stairwell, you'd best come up, *poco tiempo*. For if you don't, I can still chase her down four flights pretty good and I'm likely to be sore as hell at both of you, hear?"

The Great Costello hesitated, then asked, "What's to prevent you from rushing the stairwell and nailing both of us?"

Longarm replied in an injured tone, "Now who's doubting the word of a gent, and me a lawman instead of a damned old crook?"

The older man laughed dryly, and said, "All right. I

105

can't see any way that's as safe for all concerned. Give me three or four minutes." Then he hung up.

Longarm cradled the set at his end and told the redhead, "I reckon this is your lucky day, or night, whether you spend the rest of it pure or not."

But as he freed her wrist and hauled her to her feet she pleaded, "Don't do it, darling. I'm willing to do anything you say, anything, but they'll hang my poor father for certain!"

"Oh, I dunno. They sure screwed up the last time. I don't want you doing anything, honey. When I tell you to light out I want you to do so and, for old time's sake, I want you to put the Mighty Mississippi betwixt us as fast as you can. They hardly ever send me back east, and you might be able to get a more honest job if you really try."

Then, holding her firmly by the wrist with his left hand, he snuffed the lamp and led her through the darkness to the door. He cracked it open, didn't get shot, and drew his .44 with his free hand as he studied the dimly lit and deserted hallway as far as the stairs. Then he told the girl, "All right. It's about that time. Just start walking, not running, for the nearest exit. If I hear you running down them stairs I'll be right behind you before you can hope to reach the bottom."

She said, "Custis, he's not really an evil man. It's just that he got so tired of waiting to be recognized as the great stage illusionist he really is and—"

"Get going," Longarm cut in, pushing her out into the hall with a pat on her sweet backside that made him feel sort of wistful. She hesitated, shrugged, and started walking, not looking back. He was glad. It hurt to have anything that nice leaving angry, even when you couldn't see its face.

She got to the stairwell, stared down, then gave her red head a sort of willful fling and headed down until she was out of sight. Longarm waited a few seconds, then he growled, "All right, fool. All bets are off and why are we still standing here?"

Then another door, midway down the hall, opened all the way and the Great Costello stepped out, hands shoulder high, with a sheepish grin on his face.

Longarm stayed put as he said, "This sure is a pleasant surprise, old son. Just keep coming this way and we shall see what we shall see."

As the rogue magician joined Longarm he asked, "Did you really think I had someone else in my room with a gun, at this late stage of our little game."

Longarm hauled him inside, frisked him, shoved him down on the bed, and handcuffed Costello's clubbed foot to the brass leg of the bed. When he straightened up and relit the lamp he said, "That might have fit within the exact wording of the deal we made. But offhand I'd say it's more likely you asked for them extra moments to give the others time to move out."

The Great Costello said, "You'd make a good illusionist, given a little training in the tricks of the trade."

"You've taught me enough, for now. How come you wanted to set off all that dynamite in here, seeing you've been just across the hall all this time?"

"I just had my, uh, wife change our room to this floor, for a better view of El Paso, and you. It would have been stupid to try that telephone trick on you a second time, once we found you'd defused it. That was O'Horan's idea, by the way. As you can see, I've always felt it was smarter, as well as nicer, to stick to simple misdirection."

"Cut the bullshit. I know how you got that post office safe open. It was three of your boys, not one, who hauled Topkick Thompson out of that staged pile-up and put the noose around his neck. The fourth up there on the platform with you had to be the one as tripped the trap lever, right?"

The Great Costello shook his head and said, "You

107

weren't paying attention. O'Horan and Martin Pender-gast were all it took to help me change places and coats with that hangman. I was the one who sprung the trap. I had to, so I could drop through it and stagger away sort of dusty and confused."

"Then you admit you can kill when you think you have to?"

The older man smiled bitterly and asked, "Why not? What can you do about it, hang me?"

Longarm smiled thinly and said, "I sort of admire a gent who can face facts so philosophical. While we're on the subject, how on earth did you beat me over that rail-yard fence by such a lead, or was that someone else shooting at me to make me think I was chasing you?"

The Great Costello smiled modestly and said, "It was one of my girls. Once she had you pinned down, she only had to walk away in a ladylike way."

Longarm grimaced and said, "We figured you just walked out the front door betwixt your uniformed helpers. How did you gun the real guards so silent after luring them upstairs with three of your whores?"

The Great Costello looked hurt and replied in an injured tone, "That's not fair. I only had Maureen and one other girl in my troupe checked into the hotel. We both know why Maureen wasn't able to help, but I'm broad-minded, as long as she says she enjoyed it. The other sweet child never spread her thighs for anyone but your friend, Guilfoyle. She was able to pick up each guard in turn, drug them, and go back down for another. She had to allow the last one, Guilfoyle, a chance to remember her more fondly, as an alibi, see?"

Longarm shook his head and said, "Not hardly. Guil-foyle said the one he'd picked up was staying there with one other gal. I failed to make the connection until later. That leaves three other rooms they couldn't have been checked into. So to lure them other guards into unbooked rooms and leave 'em safely locked away to be found by that chambermaid . . ."

The Great Costello smiled smugly and said, "I could tell you, but I'd rather let you guess."

Longarm shrugged and said, "Don't have to. The chambermaid was one of your troupe. Such help is always hard to find at the wages a seedy hotel like that might offer. She got a job there, first, and that gave her pass keys and a free run of the upstairs as well as a vantage place as lookout for the others. But all the hired help there couldn't have been on your side. How did she manage to gun them three unconscious men, after the rest of us had left, without her employers noticing?"

"It's against all I stand for to give away tricks of the trade. But since I want you to know that none of the young ladies in my act are killers, I'd better confess that was Tommy O'Horan's idea, too. He did it without consulting me, since I was still in that death cell when he did it. He never shot them, he killed all three of them with the same burglar tool."

"A real sweet kid. Shoving spent bullets into the wounds with that same glorified screwdriver confused me considerable. I don't believe he wasn't told to do it, though. Like all your other razzle-dazzle, that was meant to send us sniffing one way while you made tracks the other."

The Great Costello shrugged and said, "Whatever you say and, speaking of making tracks, am I supposed to just sit here chained to this bed, or were you planning to hand me over to the authorities sooner or later?"

"I'm an authority and I got to study on that," Longarm said. "I figure you still have eight or nine arrows to your bow. Before you said nighty-night to 'em just now, for instance, you'd have mentioned that the usual way a lawman in my position would proceed would be to lock you up in the local hoosegow until I could arrange to transport you back to Colorado."

"Isn't that what you intend to do?" asked his prisoner.

"Not hardly," Longarm said. "Springing you from a patent cell again would be a lot harder, with me starting to get the hang of how you all work. But they'd likely try, and I don't want to see anyone else hurt in a fight that ain't their own."

He fished out two smokes, gave one to his prisoner, and struck a light for the both of them as he mused, "There won't be a train out for some time, and even that one's headed the wrong way. Do you have a mount stabled downstairs, seeing we seem to have picked the same hotel?"

His prisoner snorted, "Surely you jest."

Longarm said, "Thanks. I was wondering if you city dudes were in shape to chase us on horseback." Then he reached in his pocket for the handcuff key. But as he got it out, the Great Costello raised his club foot to wave sort of show-off as he said, "Don't bother."

Longarm laughed despite himself and said, "All right, get the other link off that bed leg if you're so smart." And the Great Costello simply reached down and somehow did so. Longarm knew better than to ask how. He just took the set back with a nod of thanks, hooked them to the back of his gun rig, and said, "I may as well keep 'em, anyway. You never know when you might want to cuff a more ignorant cuss. Now, get up. Slow. You may be too slick to hold with hardware, but I've yet to see a gent escape from the box once I put a round in him where it counts."

The smaller as well as older man rose politely from the bed to say, "I'm at your service, with nothing up my sleeves."

"There'd better not be. I don't expect your fellow magicians to make their play before they figure where I mean to lock you up for the night. We're going down the stairwell, now. If you try to bolt I'll kill you, and no

110

doubt many a hangman will heave a vast sigh of relief when they hear about it."

The Great Costello promised to behave and did, all the way down to the side entrance. He asked why they were entering the stable instead of leaving the hotel. Longarm told him, "Because stables are where they keep horses."

Then he frog-marched his prisoner inside, made him place both hands on the top rail of a stall, and told the surprised groom, "I'll bet you ten dollars you can't saddle and bridle my chestnut, saddle a livery nag the same way, and get us out of here in less than five minutes."

He lost. Naturally the groom wanted to know where they might be going with the horse-for-hire and naturally Longarm told him, "For a ride. You have my word you'll get your awful nag and fair saddle back. If I told you more than that you might have to lie under torture. So should anyone ask, feel free to tell 'em what you know and don't ask to know no more, hear?"

The groom said that sounded fair and wished them a safe *hasta la vista*, to wherever the hell they were going, as they rode off with Longarm covering his prisoner from the rear.

The Great Costello rode pretty good, albeit not as good as he might have on a faster mount than Longarm's. After they'd ridden a few city blocks, the prisoner turned in his saddle to ask, "Did you have some particular destination in mind or am I just supposed to guess?"

Longarm said, "Swing east at the next corner. I'm taking you out to Fort Bliss. Your playmates will play hell busting you out of an army guardhouse once I tell the army what a distinguished federal prisoner I want 'em to sit on for a spell."

"I might have expected you to be so sneaky. What then, a choo-choo back to Colorado?"

"If I wanted you to know my plans in advance I'd tell

'em to you. So let's talk about something else. No offense, but for such a ferocious Irishman you don't talk so Irish. How come?"

The Great Costello sighed and said, "My people brought me to the States as a kid. You must have heard about the great potato blight of the forties. The reason my daughters sound even more American is that their mother, God rest her, was raised on this side of the water as well."

Longarm didn't comment on the slip. Knowing Maureen had at least one sister among the clan could come in handy if she failed to heed his sincere advice about going straight, as well as east, before he had time to look for her again.

They'd ridden but a short way out of town when, somewhere in the darkness, Longarm heard a polite but sinister voice call out, *"Hey, amigo, a'onde va?"*

Longarm reined in, ordered his prisoner to do the same, and called back, "I wish you'd cut that out, El Gato. It's spooky enough when a man ain't on the prod. Why can't you just meet folk natural on the trail like everyone else?"

A mounted black shadow detached itself from some mesquite trees just off the wagon trace and came to join them. El Gato even had his damn fool mount trained to move like a big old cat. Closer in, he turned into a nice-looking young gent with features more Spanish than Indian, even thought he was said to be meaner than a drunk Apache if one crossed him. As usual, the Mexican desperado was wearing a big black sombrero and black charro outfit to match his big black horse. Where some might have sported silver braid and conchos, El Gato preferred big ebony buttons and no braid at all. He said, "It is not my custom to be seen before I decide whether to speak or shoot. Since you have your gun out, and I still hope we are old friends, is it safe to assume you are riding with a prisoner tonight?"

Longarm said, "It is. El Gato, I want you to meet the Great Costello. You two have a lot in common—you're both spooky as hell."

El Gato nodded pleasantly at the older man, but told Longarm, "Shoot him. Can't you see he is trying to escape?"

Longarm replied, "Not at the moment. I'm taking him out to the fort to see if we can't break him of that habit."

El Gato shook his head and said, "We don't have time. We have to ride, *amigo*. Tonight *los rurales* came over the border and grabbed Don Julio Valdez, on Americano soil! The offspring of dead dogs and sex-mad toads have no shame about such matters!"

Longarm whistled softly and said, "I was wondering what all that fuss at the fiesta was about. If it's any comfort, I got one of them *rurales* for your folk."

El Gato chuckled and said, "Oh, was that you? We were wondering who might have gotten the third one. But that is neither here nor there. They have Don Julio, back in Ciudad Juarez, and now we must save him, *amigo*."

Longarm owed El Gato. They'd long since lost track of who'd saved who the most often. So his voice was sincere as he told the worried young rebel, "I'd like to help but I can't. Three reasons. No, forget the part about Billy Vail ordering me to stay the hell out of Mexico. That still leaves two. I got this prisoner on my hand, and by now Don Julio can't hardly be just over the river in Juarez. Anyone *El Presidente* hates that much is surely on his way to Mexico City by now."

El Gato shook his head again. He did that good with such a big sombrero. He said, "Your prisoner is no problem if you have any bullets in that gun. If you do not, allow me to nail him as he attempts to get away. No? Then allow me to point out there is no way for the triple-titted *rurales* to take Don Julio south, right now.

113

That unusual weather we just had swept away a railroad trestle just south of Juarez, so they'll have to hold him there until the trains can run again. And despite what you may have heard about my people, the track crews work fast, as only a peon with a *rurale* standing over him with a gun can work."

Longarm hesitated. El Gato was not the sort of man who'd remind another man about a little thing like saving his life in the past. But he was upset enough to insist, "They'll kill him, Longarm. That sadist in power will enjoy the show of giving Don Julio a fair trial. Diaz loves to kill his enemies with a display of stern fatherly remorse. As an officer, Diaz was in charge when they executed Maximillian; it was his idea to have the band play "La Paloma," knowing it was the doomed man's favorite Mexican song, and that he'd never hear the end of it."

Longarm said, "Damn it, you know what I think of that oily bastard down in Mexico City. I'll tell you what —help me get this other oily bastard out to Fort Bliss and I'll ride with you for Juarez, even though we only figure to get your pal, Valdez, killed earlier, likely along with you and me."

El Gato insisted, "The fort's too far, and in the wrong direction. We don't have enough time as it is. Why can't you just shoot this *cabrón*, like an old *compañero?*"

Longarm said, "He ain't my old *compañero*. Even if he was, that ain't my style. I said I'd help if I could, pard. But first I got to make sure of this rascal. Maybe better than I planned on, as I'm likely fixing to die in Mexico on another fool's errand. You know damn well the two of us ain't about to spring Don Julio out of no Mexican jail with him surrounded by at least a company of *rurales* on the prod."

Before El Gato could answer, the Great Costello

114

said, "You're right, Longarm, the two of you couldn't. But the three of us just might."

El Gato asked Longarm, "Hey, why is this one talking so wild?"

Longarm explained, "He's an escape artist. He knows more than he's supposed to about busting folk out of jail. But you're right. He's talking wild."

"Am I? Are you suggesting a bunch of Mexicans who've never heard of me would be better at guarding a prisoner than you American feds I made monkeys out of just a few weeks ago?"

El Gato said, "You see? He insults your country. Shoot him."

But Longarm said, "That wouldn't be fair. He did make us all look like monkeys. But I dunno. Aiding and abetting a Mexican uprising on my own, against orders, sounds bad enough. Enlisting the help of a convicted murderer sounds just plain silly."

El Gato shot a thoughtful look at the Great Costello and asked, "Is he really that good? Do you think he could help Don Julio escape before the trains are running again?"

"He's billed as an escaping wonder, on or off the stage," Longarm said. "I'm wondering just who's escape we're talking about right now, though."

The Great Costello said, "I don't think I'd want to be an outlaw in Mexico. I don't speak the lingo and I can't abide the food and water. But you'll never get your pal out of Mexico without my help."

Longarm said, "He ain't my pal. But if Diaz wants him dead he can't be all bad. Why do you want to save him, Costello? What's in it for you?"

His prisoner shrugged and asked, "A sporting chance?"

"You know I can't just let you go. Can't you do no better than that?"

"Here's my deal. I help you two save Valdez, no

tricks, until we all agree he's safe. Then you and I shoot it out man to man and, win or lose, I won't have to hang."

El Gato said, "Take him up on it, Longarm. Nobody can beat you in a fair fight!"

"You ain't seen this old boy move with his hands cuffed and a hangman's hood over his fool face. Even if he was a mite less deadly, I ain't sure it would be lawful. Out-and-out dueling has been outlawed for some time in every state I know of."

The Great Costello suggested, "We could have it out in Mexico, where there are no laws at all, if you insist on being picky. Suppose I give you my word I'll work with you until your young friend here has Valdez safely out of Mexico. Then the two of us can settle the matter as men of honor."

Longarm asked, "With what? I'd be a fool to let you get your hands on a gun, even to rescue Don Julio."

The prisoner nodded and said, "I probably won't need one to misdirect the *rurales*. But do I have your word I can have one, when the time comes?"

"That's a mighty tall order," Longarm said. "I'd have to study on it, some."

El Gato snapped, "Think about it as we ride, then. *Vamanos, compañeros!* Let's go kill some *rurales* before we worry about killing one another, damn it!"

They paused in the El Paso Mexican Quarter long enough to outfit Longarm and the Great Costello with charro jackets and less gringo sombreros. Then came the less amusing task of fording the Rio Grande, or Rio Bravo; it was a bitch by whatever name one wanted to call it.

During more usual late summer weather, the river was shallow enough for domestic help in El Paso to cross on foot, regular. But thanks to the recent rain the river was a brawling flood. They had to swim their

mounts across and, as Longarm helped both the Great
Costello and his livery stable nag buck the current, he
was glad El Gato had argued him out of returning the
ten dollar plug and mounting the magician on something
more seaworthy. He almost lost both of them, and while
drowning the Great Costello sounded fair, he'd have had
to pay for a more expensive horse out of his own
pocket. He'd no doubt owe the livery extra, in any case,
if they didn't make this trip to Mexico short and sweet.

In hopes of doing that, they rode into Ciudad Juarez
from the east, lest someone mistake them for Apache in
the darkness. Like El Paso, Juarez consisted of a com-
pact inner city surrounded by more sprawling suburbs.
Mex 'dobes sprawled better than the frame housing
most Anglo-Texicans preferred. A mess of dogs fussed
at them as they rode in, but there were no street lamps,
so nothing the dog owners threw at them came close
enough to worry about.

The hour was late, but since most Mexicans slept the
heat of day away in order to work and play at night, the
narrow streets of downtown Juarez were crowded and,
again, they had that shifty romantic light to move about
in. Longarm and of course El Gato could answer questions thrown at them in Spanish, so they had the Great
Costello ride between them. Longarm told him to just
shrug and sort of sigh, *"Quien sabe?"* if he couldn't get
out of talking to someone. While it literally means,
"Who knows?" it could mean "None of your damn business," "I don't feel like talking to you," or "Leave me
the hell alone." It was better to be taken for rude and
surly than for a gringo in Ciudad Juarez after dark.

El Gato led them to a *posada* he knew of, near Police
Headquarters and across the street from the bullring.
They only held bullfights on Sunday afternoons, so they
didn't have to worry about the blank brick wall across
the way. The innkeeper El Gato was no doubt related to
said he'd worry about their mounts, and suggested

117

they'd feel more comfortable if they ate upstairs instead of with the other guests, since at least two of the sons of unwashed nuns and depraved priests were police informers.

As the three of them moved up the dark stairs the Great Costello protested that he wasn't hungry. Longarm explained, "I ain't, neither, but never miss a chance to bust bread with a Mex. It makes him feel like a real shit if he has to turn on you."

El Gato knew where they were supposed to wind up. He led them into a corner suite that smelled like corn husks and old wasp nests, and threw open the jalousied doors leading out onto a balcony. He pointed across the mostly flat rooftops at a dark mass rising a story higher and growled, "That is the *rurale* outpost we have to break into and out of."

The Great Costello asked, "How do you know?"

Before the young Mex could hit him Longarm said, "That's a fair question. *Los rurales* are a sort of highway patrol, not city police. Don Julio could just as easily be in the civil jail, here, you know."

El Gato shrugged and said, "Or the army garrison, if those raiders turned him over to *los federales*. I see the point. You two wait here while I take a stroll among my people, eh?"

Longarm knew better than to try to stop El Gato. He never sounded too serious, but he never said anything he didn't mean. So he was alone with the Great Costello, a few minutes later, when a short, plump but pretty *mestiza* brought them a huge tray piled with chicken, rice, beans and pulque. The only thing they hadn't put too much pepper in was the booze.

She asked where El Gato was, and when Longarm assured her he'd be back she sighed and said, "I hope it shall be before his food grows cold. It is such a great honor for to cook for a hero of the people."

Longarm reassured her and she left. As he and the

Great Costello sat on the floor of the balcony with the tray between them, the magician took an experimental bite, grimaced, and said, "This stuff couldn't get cold if you put it in an ice house in January. What's this stuff in the clay cups? It smells something like flat beer and tastes like warm spit?"

Longarm chuckled and said, "It's fermented cactus juice. Not as strong as tequila, but go easy on it, anyway. Pulque is the poor man's beer in these parts and leads to more blood and slaughter than one might suspect from the uninteresting taste. I don't know if it's stronger than our suds or whether they get drunk easier. It could be both."

The Great Costello said he could never drink enough of it to get drunk and asked about the bullring across the way. Longarm said, "We don't figure on being here long enough to worry about all the whooping and hollering next Sunday. I've never figured out why they hold *La Fiesta Brava* on the sabbath, since it don't strike me as a religious experience. On the other hand, it's always struck me as a lot of trouble to go to any time when the end result is a stabbed cow."

"Do they ever hold bullfights at night?" asked the greener-to-Mexico man.

Longarm laughed and said, "Not to my knowledge. Some of them fighting bulls can get sort of dangerous, even when you can see 'em coming at you in broad-ass daylight. Why are we talking about bullfights, old son?"

"You just said the locals find them exciting. Excited people cause confusion, right?"

"I follow your drift, but like I said, they don't figure on attracting a bullfight crowd over yonder this side of Sunday afternoon."

The Great Costello asked, "What about fireworks? Do you think it would be possible to buy some fireworks this late after the Fourth of July?"

"Hell, if you got the money you can buy a six-year-old virgin in Juarez, or at least they'll tell you she's a virgin. Fireworks are easier. They don't take the Fourth of July as serious as we do, but Mexicans do shoot off fireworks at Christmas. Your drift is getting easier to follow and it sounds like fun. I knew a bank robber one time who liked to cover up his gunplay with strings of Chinese firecrackers. I felt sort of morose, having to gun such a playful cuss. What else do you reckon we'll need to misdirect the audience, old son?"

The rogue magician said, "I'm still thinking. I don't know just what the trick will have to be, yet. It depends on where and how they're holding the rabbit I mean to vanish."

They went on talking and poking at the grub for a spell. Longarm got to know his prisoner better, but didn't like him any better, as the Great Costello boasted of great illusions he'd invented, and displayed a good bit of self-pity in the process.

When he was able to slip a word in edgewise, Longarm said to Costello, "You're full of shit. You may know more than me about putting on a magic act, but I know something about watching 'em. It's small wonder you made your small-time audiences yawn, if you went through all that fuss to make your daughter Maureen climb into one truck and pop out of another on the far side of the stage. It's like I just said about *La Fiesta Brava*—unless you're really up on the finer points, you have to watch a gent in a monkey suit take forever, prancing and dancing, before he just gets down to butchering some beef like you expected him to from the beginning. What in thunder would your audience expect a redhead in a rainy-suzie skirt to do when she climbed into a trunk except to vanish, or at least turn into something else? What would anyone expect to leap out of the second truck but the same pretty gal, an elephant? You might have done better if you'd worked faster. All them

120

drumrolls and brags gave your audience time to figure out what was coming."

The Great Costello scowled and said, "All right. You're not the first to complain that my timing might have been a bit off. But damn it, that was a good trick. Not even the managers who told me my act was slowly paced could ever tell me how I did it!"

"They must not have been as interested in magic as me, then. I spend lots of time at the Denver Library, reading up on all sorts of stuff. A man in my line of work can't know too much, and I once made a fool out of a dangerous medicine man by knowing more than most old boys about electric wiring. He had a big old electromagnet rigged so only him and his friends looked strong enough to pick up an iron anvil. He sure looked dumb, once I done some rewiring."

"All right, suppose you tell me how I dematerialized Maureen in one place and made her appear in another," Costello challenged.

"Well, I ain't no infernal magician, but even I know how easy it is to make any number of trunks look empty if you have a mirror in 'em at a forty-five degree angle. With the lid open, the glass reflecting the side that ain't covered by it makes it look as if one's looking in at both sides—adding up to empty—when you still got half the space to hide things or folk in."

The stage magician grumbled, "There ought to be a law against printing books like that. If you're so smart, how did I get her clean across the stage to the other trunk without anyone seeing her travel a foot?"

"She didn't have to get out of the first box," Longarm said. "She just had to scrunch up under the hinged mirror so you could prove it was empty. The gal who got out of the second box, after acting invisible the same way, was no doubt her twin, or at least a sister close enough to pass for her at that range."

The Great Costello stared across at Longarm, thun-

121

dergasted, to demand, "Did she tell you that? I mean, fun is fun, but she had no right to give away trade secrets to a rube!"

Longarm soothed, "She never. You did. You slipped up and let me know you had at least two daughters. The notion they might be twins only came to me when you bragged on how you could make redheads fly through the air, invisible. When something don't strike me as possible, I generally try to figure out what might be."

The Great Costello sighed and said, "It's just as well I gave up show business, if even cowboys can get at books published by traitors. But let me tell you about an illusion I pulled off in Toledo, one time. It was a one-of-kind, because the theatre had an unusual design, but . . ."

Then El Gato came back and Longarm was spared the brag. The young Mex hunkered down with them and said, "They don't have Don Julio where we thought. They had already taken him to the railroad depot when word came in about that washed-out trestle. The special detail holding him works out of Ciudad Méjico, not here. So they simply bundled him upstairs in the hotel by the depot. Naturally, the arrogant bastards don't have to worry about hotel bills. Had they not evicted guests to take over a luxury suite for their own use, I would have had more trouble finding all of this out."

Longarm grimaced and said, "I'd say you found out good and bad. Getting in might be easier, but that hotel's smack in the middle of town, with bright lights all around, save for the rail yards behind the depot, that is."

El Gato said, "Sí, I think our best escape route would lie in that direction, too."

But the Great Costello objected, "So will they. And you said there's a railroad crew working, under military guard, just to the south of those tracks. I like the front door better."

Longarm told El Gato, "That's how he walked out of the Denver House of Detention. Of course, to walk anybody out of any door we got to get him out of that top-floor suite, first. How far up are we talking, El Gato?"

"Six stories."

"Ouch. A six-story running gunfight down a stairwell might not be all that bad if there was some way to avoid a reception committee at the bottom. No handy rooftops we might be able to scamper across?"

El Gato shook his head and said, "The hotel is the most imposing edifice in that part of town. Perhaps if we spliced our reatas together . . . ?"

Longarm said, "I don't carry a throw-rope on my old army saddle, and even if I did that's just too damn far to dangle with gents shooting at you in the full glare of city lights. Do they ever turn the lights any lower in downtown Juarez?"

"*Sí*, at sunrise. My people are more casual than your own about bedtime. Some go to bed and others get up, as the spirit moves them. But the city never sleeps, unless one wants to count the afternoon siesta, of course."

"We can't afford to wait that long," Longarm said. "I for one would feel chagrined as hell if they loaded Valdez aboard a morning train after making me ride all this way." He turned to the Great Costello and said, "You seem awfully quiet for a man who delights in doing the impossible, old son."

The sly little magician sort of smirked and said, 'I have a couple of ideas. It depends on what I can find to work with."

He turned to El Gato to ask, "Can you get us some extra stooges to plant in the audience?"

Longarm had to explain that before El Gato said, "If I had my regular gang with me I would not have had to ask Longarm here to help me. Many here in Juarez love me, as well they should, since I rob from the rich and

123

give to the poor, within reason. But I could not ask any of these *pobrecito* townsmen to ride against the government with us. If they had the balls, we would have a different government."

"We don't need anyone to risk his neck," the magician said. "We only need more confusion than any three men could hope to stir up, see?"

El Gato nodded and said, "Oh, one can always arrange a riot after dark in Ciudad Juarez."

"Good. Now it's time to do some shopping. I know we'll need some stopwatches, or at least some cheap watches that keep time for say, an hour or so, without losing track by more than a few minutes. I'm sure about the fireworks. I'll cross the other bridges when you get me to them. Let's go."

El Gato rose, but told Longarm, "You'd better wait here. He'll need me to speak Spanish for him. The three of us, together, may attract more than fireworks, no?"

Longarm considered. It would have been a waste of time to tell El Gato to keep a sharp eye on Costello. El Gato was called "The Cat" because his sharp eyes didn't miss much, even in the dark. So he nodded and contented himself with saying, "Don't come back without him. What time are we likely talking about, Costello?"

"Hard to say, before I see the merchandise. If we're not back by midnight, start without us."

Longarm waited until they'd left before he fished out his pocketwatch, struck a match, and read it as going on ten. He hadn't wanted the little rascal to suspect he didn't know just everything.

He finished his pulque and got up to wander back inside. The only furniture worth sitting on seemed to be the bunks against the 'dobe walls. He sat on one. The mattress was stuffed with corn husks and sounded like it. He tossed his hat and coat aside, crunched his back to the wall, and settled down to wait a spell, wishing he had something to read, or at least that he wasn't sitting on a fire hazard.

He'd about decided to go ahead and smoke, anyway, when the plump little *mestiza* came in for the tray. He waved her on out to the balcony, and when she came back in with it she told him he should be ashamed for to leave so much on his plate when people were starving all over Mexico. He smiled up at her and asked, "What happens if I swallow another bean? Does a kid in Yucatan sit up and burp?"

She laughed and left, if only for a little while. He'd just finished a cheroot, decided it tasted awful on top of pepper and pulque, and gotten rid of it when the *mestiza* came back, with nothing but herself to offer. He suspected that had to be what she was offering—he saw she'd changed her blouse for a clean one two sizes too small and smelled the rose perfume in her hair. But it wasn't considered polite to just throw a gal down and tear her duds off, even in Juarez. So she got to sit down beside him and jaw about *la revolución* and how brave he was to help El Gato save her people. He decided it was time to mention that El Gato would be back around midnight, and that they'd all be leaving soon after if she was really feeling dedicated to *la revolución*.

She said she sure was and that he might have warned her sooner that he'd be riding off to battle any time now. Then she asked him to help her with the buttons on the back of her blouse and, one thing leading to another, they were making a hell of a racket atop those corn husks before they got around to each other's names. She said she was called Felicidad and that she was a virgin, when it came to Anglos. He'd figured she had a healthy curiosity about such matters when she first went down on him before he could get his pants off.

Felicidad seemed grateful as well as surprised when he pounded her to glory the second time. But when he

125

left it in she sighed, kissed him regretfully, and said she had other guests to take care of.

Since she'd never mentioned money, he assumed she hadn't meant that the way it could be taken, although, considering her warm and willing nature, anything was possible.

He watched her dress up innocent, standing over him in the soft dim light, and while it made a pretty picture, he couldn't help wondering what she really looked like.

She bent over to kiss him a fond farewell, and then she was gone and he was getting dressed again himself. He had to chuckle as he considered what the others might have said if they'd come back early.

He got out his watch, lit another match, and marveled, "Hell, it's already after midnight. Ain't it a caution how time flies when you're having a good time?"

Then he rose and began to pace back and forth, starting to worry about what he'd tell Billy Vail if the Great Costello had escaped again, or whether he was going to live or not, if the sneaky rascal had something else planned for this evening.

Chapter 15

When they finally did return, just as Longarm was about to go looking for them, he was mighty glad old Felicidad had turned out to be so cold-natured. For they were not alone—El Gato had enlisted a whole posse of young Mexicans. Half of 'em were carrying bags of stuff the Great Costello had picked up at south-of-the-border prices.

Just the same, he'd spent more than twenty dollars, U.S., and thought Longarm ought to reimburse him.

Longarm told him not to be silly and asked what all the stuff was good for. So Costello said, "Misdirection. They may find some use for the two-bit watches and bugle, later."

"You bought a bugle, too?"

El Gato said, "We have been very busy—you were so right about this one moving fast. These *muchachos* have their own instructions. Now it is time for us to go meet the girls."

Longarm gulped and said, "Hold on, I never come

all the way down here to get laid, even though sometimes things don't work out as planned."

The Great Costello explained, "Not those kinds of girls. Our handsome young friend here has recruited three reasonably respectable-looking dance-hall gals to go along with the act. Come on, they're waiting for us downstairs in the carriage."

Longarm shrugged and went along with the act, whatever it might be.

Downstairs, he found that, sure enough, three not-bad giggling gals were seated in this closed carriage the others had hired. It would have been close enough with all six of them piled in—all the cheap luggage the Great Costello had picked up as well made it worse—but at least one of the Mex gals needed a bath.

But the drive to the depot hotel was mercifully swift, and as he helped the one he was supposed to be with down from the carriage, he could tell from her hairy armpit that she was not the really stinky one. He still felt sort of red-faced as the six of them walked into the lobby, bold as brass, and El Gato hired three adjoining rooms for them. Longarm assumed the luggage was meant to make it look less indecent. But from the smirk on the room clerk's face, it hadn't.

They couldn't get rooms on the top floor. The ones they got on the fifth, however, were almost under the suite they were holding Valdez in, overlapping by one room, according to El Gato. The rooms the conspirators had booked separate could be turned into a suite by opening some inside doors, with Longarm's lock-pick blade—so that's what they did. The girls asked how come, as one of them bounced playfully on a bed and asked who she was with. El Gato told her to shut up and be serious.

The Great Costello opened a hatbox he'd carried in and took out a more sedate black dress as he told El Gato, "Oh, let her have fun. She's going to have to take

128

that red satin dress off anyway, and if you don't want to enjoy the experience, I can't say when I'll ever get a chance to get laid again."

Longarm said, "Hold on, damn it. This surely is a lot of fuss if you mean to stage an orgy, Costello. Can't you ever do anything plain and simple?"

"I'm not sure just what I mean to do, yet." Then he opened a closet door, laughed like a mean little kid, and said, "Oh, yes, perfect! I hoped this would be an up-to-date as well as first-class railroad hotel!"

Longarm stared over his shoulder at the full-length mirror stuck to the inside of the door where guests of fashion could make sure they were dressed right before going out. He started to ask what all the fuss was about, then he gasped and said, "Oh, shit. A magic box yards away on the far side of the footlights may be one thing, but now you're really talking foolish."

The Great Costello took out his watch as he observed, "It won't work unless your pal, Valdez, has plenty of nerve. You're going to need even more." Then he told them the plan.

When he'd finished Longarm and El Gato were staring at each other soberly, and the three girls were crying and pleading with them not to talk so scary.

El Gato sighed and said, "I do not enjoy staring down from trees any more than any other cat, but you are the stronger of the two of us. Plus, I am wearing black, and Valdez knows me."

Longarm didn't argue. His palms were sweating just thinking about it. The Great Costello said, "You two work that part out as you go along. Could I borrow that pocketknife, Longarm? We haven't much time and the screws holding this big mirror look a bit rusty."

They weren't. As the nimble-fingered little man removed the mirror from the door he warned, "Don't drop it. It may be the only one." So Longarm was careful as he took the big fragile sheet of glass from him.

El Gato already had his coil of braided reata handy. He said, *"Bueno,* let's get up to the roof, *poco tiempo.* I understand the part about the bullring."

Longarm wished he'd spent all that time with the Great Costello. He could only carry the fool mirror as El Gato led the way, rope in one hand and drawn gun in the other.

They made the stairwell without incident.

Then they were up on the roof. Even away from the edge it seemed higher than Longarm felt the last time he'd been up in the capital dome in Denver. They moved over to the edge above their own hired rooms and, they hoped, the ones Julio Valdez was being held in. Longarm leaned the big mirror against the parapet and said, "Well, we'd best rig an ass-sling for you, old son. Are you sure you know how this trick with a mirror works?"

El Gato said, "I think so. I just shove Don Julio in the closet and place the mirror over him, no?"

"You don't know how it works," Longarm said. Then he moved over to a vent pipe and fastened one end of the reata snuggly to the rusty iron. He gave it a couple of tugs and said, "That ought to hold me. I'll never speak to you again if it don't."

El Gato protested, *"Pero no,* I won't be able to haul you back up, you moose."

"I know," Longarm said. "Why don't you run back down and make sure my prisoner don't escape? If he was half as smart as me, he'd know this is a one-man job, and he just may be."

El Gato said he wanted to watch, at least. But Longarm told him to go on down.

Longarm took a deep breath, got as good a hold as he could on the glass with one hand, and backed off the roof holding on to the reata with the other. He'd never have been able to slide down so easily if it hadn't been oiled and braided rawhide. As it was, he almost slid past the sixth-story sill, and caught it with his boots just in time. This left him hanging just outside the window. It was lucky the window wasn't nailed shut, and even luckier that the only man inside was Don Julio. The Mexican politician looked mighty surprised when Longarm tapped on a bottom pane with his toe. But he was too smart to shout out loud as he rolled off the bed, came over, and opened the window inwards, whispering, "Who are you, aside from an obvious lunatic, I mean?"

Longarm swung on in, mirror and all, and as he dropped to the rug, whispered back, "I'm glad your English is so much better than my Spanish. We ain't got time to talk. Do just what I say, even if you think it's crazy, and there's a hundred-to-one chance we'll get you out of this fix, alive."

The older man said, "That's a better chance than they will offer at my so-called trial in Ciudad Méjico. What is it you wish for me to do?"

Longarm glanced about for a handy closet, spied a tall but skinny cedar wardrobe he liked even better and told the Mexican to climb in.

Then he wedged Don Julio in one corner, standing atop the bottom drawers under the hang-up space, and offered a few words of terse explanation as he wedged the mirror in between them at an angle. He said, "You'll have to grip the top edge with your fingertips to hold this steady. But they ought to be shaded by the hanger-rod along with the top edge. Now hold that pose and not a peep out of you until I come back to haul you out of there personal."

He stepped back to view his handywork and muttered, "Shit."

Don Julio asked what was wrong. Longarm said, "That was a peep. I told you not to do that." Then he shifted the mirror until it was only bouncing the image of dark cedarwood out at him, and got rid of the clothes

131

hanger that was messing up the illusion with an oddly angled twin. He said, "I'm going to leave this door wide open and shut the closet. There's more call to peer sharp into something you have to open. Pay no attention to all the noise you're about to hear, and remember nobody can see you no matter how much they're yelling at you."

He turned away, shut the closet door, and trimmed the only lamp in the room low and shadow-casting, but not all the way out.

He'd no sooner done so when a side door opened and a *rurale* came in muttering something, then froze with his jaw hanging open when he saw how Don Julio had suddenly grown so tall. It was not the best way to be standing when anything as big as Longarm was throwing a left hook.

He nailed the *rurale* on the button. His victim dropped with no more fight in him, and little more noise than a wet dishrag. Longarm left the door ajar beyond the *rurale's* boot heels and ran over to the window to grab the reata in both hands and start climbing. The height didn't bother him as much now, as he considered what it might feel like to get shot right up the ass.

But he made it to the roof, rolled over the parapet, and made it to the stairwell just as somewhere in the distance a tinny bugle blew an after-midnight invitation to the bullfight. Then the skies above Ciudad Juarez began to light up red, white, green, and purple as the first skyrockets commenced exploding.

From the point of view of the *rurales* who thought they were holding Valdez overnight in a safe place, the festivities seemed even more confusing. Attracted by the noise outside, three of them ran into the prisoner's murky room, almost tripped over their unconscious comrade, and added to the confusion by yelling a lot and bumping into one another as they tried to cover all bets at once. Their sergeant joined them, demanding to

132

know what in the hell they were fussing about, in the harsh tones only a topkick with a parade-ground roar could muster. The *rurale* who'd opened the closet door roared back, "The *cabrón* is not here!" just as the one peering under the bed got back to his feet to groan, *"Nada!* But where could he have gone?"

The sergeant swept a casual eye around the dimly lit but all too obviously vacated premises, including the gaping door of the obviously empty wardrobe, and snapped, "The window is open!"

The *rurale* closest to them stuck his head out and said, "I found it! He used a rope for to climb down!"

The smarter sergeant shoved him out of the way, stared morosely down at the milling crowd in the street far below, and shouted, "Not down, up! The line is only hanging a few meters below this sill. Get out to the stairs before he makes it down from the roof!"

All of them but the one helping the dazed man on the rug tore out of the room, guns drawn. The one Longarm had knocked galley-west was muttering, "What happened? I remember coming in to check on the prisoner and then everything went black. I think I am going to puke."

His buddy replied, "Not if you do not enjoy standing against walls you won't, Hernan. The prisoner has escaped. On your feet and help us find him if you value your life! Someone shall have to pay for this if he gets away, and between you and me, Hernan, I'd say you were it!"

He helped his dazed comrade to his feet and hauled him in the wake of the others. By this time they were on the roof, but all they could see up there was a fireworks display. They could hear it as well. Above the noise of exploding skyrockets the sergeant roared, "That makes no sense. I have lived more than forty years and in all that time I never heard of a bullfight at night."

133

One of his men said, "Just the same, they're shooting off all that stuff near the bullring, if not in it."

Their leader snapped, "That's what I just said. Corporal Gomez, take half the detail over to the Plaza del Toros and arrest whoever you find there. The rest of you follow me. We must search this hotel from top to bottom!"

They did, with the rough skills *los rurales* were notorious for, albeit without their usual needless brutality.

Longarm, El Gato, and the Great Costello were expecting to get caught in bed with red-faced women, in three separate beds. Other hotel guests were more surprised, made more of a fuss, and some of them wound up naked on the floor, with bruises, as *los rurales* looked under every bed and in every closet. But they didn't have time to rape even the pretty female guests during their frantic sweep of so many rooms.

Downstairs, they slapped the hotel help around just enough to determine they had no sensible suggestions to offer. The sergeant clanged his spurred boots out the front entrance, stared in bewilderment at the passing crowd, and grabbed an excited youth to ask where everyone was going. The kid laughed and said, "I don't know. They seem to be holding a fiesta over that way. I want to see if any pretty *muchachas* will be there."

The burly *rurale* leader let him go with a cuff across the back of his head and stomped back inside, roaring, "The whole town has gone *loco en la cabeza,* or perhaps some friends of Valdez are trying to be clever. Hernan and Quico, stand guard here and make sure the old fox can't get out the front way. Robles and Castro, get to the back exit on the double and make sure it is locked as well as guarded."

The dazed Hernan said, "I have to sit down. I am going to puke if I don't. Where are you going, Sergeant?"

His leader said, "Out to make some arrests, if we can

134

get through that damned mob. Sit down if you must, I don't see how he could still be anywhere in the building. But if he is, and you let him escape again, you won't have to worry about your weak stomach, you poor stupid *cabrón!*"

Then he waved his drawn .45 at the others and charged out into the jam-packed street, pistol-whipping a path through the crowd.

The two men remaining in the lobby moved over to an overstuffed chair with a potted palm sprouting above it. The *rurale* Longarm had left in a dazed but meditative mood sank down in the soft seat, lowered his head to his knees, and moaned, "He can't fool me. I know where he's going."

His comrade asked where and Hernan said, *"Los Estados Unidos.* That's where I am going as soon as I feel up to riding again. *El Presidente* will never be satisfied with standing less than the whole detail against the wall if that bastard gets away."

His comrade sighed and replied, *"Es verdad.* But the night is still young and how far could he have gotten by this time?"

Don Julio Valdez had in fact never left the wardrobe in the room where they'd been holding him. But as the upper stories of the hotel returned to normal, Longarm rolled out of the bed he'd been sharing, platonically, with the fair dance-hall gal called Rosalinda, and told her to get dressed. She said she would but added, with a hurt look, she'd seldom been in bed with a man who didn't even remove his gun rig.

Longarm laughed and cracked the door ajar. He saw the coast was clear, but made good use of his gun rig as he went upstairs to get Valdez out of that wardrobe. He told the Mexican to carry the mirror and stick tight. When Valdez asked how come Longarm explained, "If we mount that glass back where we found it they'll never figure out how we did it."

Valdez said that sounded fair and they were soon downstairs with the others. The middle-aged but macho Valdez put up more of an argument when the Great Costello ordered him into the red satin dress and black lace mantilla another lady had been wearing when she checked in. Longarm told him, "Do it. When three gents check into a hotel dressed sort of casual, with three gals dressed sort of cheap and flashy—no offense, *señoritas*—nobody expects 'em to spend more than an hour or so upstairs. The management knows that it won't be long before more serious lawmen are asking questions about every guest in this hotel, so they ought to be only too happy to see you leaving with El Gato, little darling."

Valdez said he understood, even if he didn't like it, and just plain refused to take off his pants. El Gato turned to the gal who'd exchanged her red dress for dowdy black and told her, "You must go with God, now, my little patriot. It is important that they see you leaving alone, with no connection to us as far as they can see, if they notice you at all."

She asked what would happen to her if they did, and El Gato told her he would burn a candle for her and someday her name might be inscribed on a monument to all the brave ones who'd laid down their lives for Mexico. She laughed, gallantly, said she doubted there'd be room enough on any one slab of marble, and moved to the door. Longarm saluted her, even though she was the one who needed a bath the most.

They gave her a good five minutes. By this time they had Don Julio passing for a mighty thick-waisted and flat-assed dance-hall gal, if nobody looked too close. The Great Costello, nearest the window, said, "There went the last volley of skyrockets. Things will soon be getting back to normal. We'd better go for it, now."

They did. They sweated bullets going down all those

136

stairs, but as they crossed the lobby they saw one of the *rurales* posted there barely glanced their way and his pal, bent over in a chair, never even looked up. The desk clerk didn't even want to notice them and ignored the keys Longarm tossed on the counter top.

They were across the crowded main street and heading up an alley Longarm might not have noticed if El Gato hadn't been in the lead with the disguised Don Julio. Once they were deeper into the dark stinky maze, the man they'd rescued began to strip off the female duds, saying, *"Bueno.* Where do we mount up for some riding, *amigos?"*

El Gato said, "We don't. The horses we rode down on are safe enough where they are and not likely to inform on us. By this time the small detail that was holding you will have enlisted *la policia ciudad* and *los federales.* They will have roadblocks set up all around, and there are few places one can cross the Rio Bravo when it's in flood."

Valdez protested, "Damn it, we can't just stay here."

El Gato told him, "I know. That is why we are on our way to the house of ill repute these girls work for. The first floor is a big cantina. The second floor is lined with cribs. Few *rurales* or *federales* who come in for to get drunk or laid could know there is a third story, above the cribs, see?"

The rescued Mexican laughed but asked, "Are you sure we can trust women who enjoy sex with the enemy?"

Rosalinda, clinging to Longarm's arm, sniffed indignantly and said, "Shame on you. How can we enjoy it when they never pay?"

Her comrade in *amor* added, *"Sí,* we fight for a free country where nobody gets to screw a woman *por nada* unless she really likes him."

So the four men and their two patriotic ladies of the

evening made their way through the inky maze, guided by El Gato's amazing night vision, to the last place *los rurales* might search for them. The attic of their favorite whorehouse.

Chapter 16

"What is the matter with you?" asked Rosalinda in the privacy of her own quarters under the sloping roof. "Do you scorn me because of the business I'm in, or are you one of those men who prefers young boys?"

Longarm chuckled as he reclined on one elbow aboard the one item of furniture there was in the tiny room, the sleeping mat, and said, "Land's sake, Rosalinda, we just crept up the back stairs with the whole place crawling with the law."

She hugged her knees at the far end of the mat to insist, "Pooh, the madam says all the lawmen in town are out looking for you *caballeros*. This floor is solid and we have no bedsprings for to worry about. I can understand your coldness back at that hotel—I confess I was worried myself—but we got away as planned and, damn it, all this excitement has made me feel most passionate."

Longarm knew himself well enough to guess he might be feeling more like celebrating if he hadn't spent an hour or so, earlier, with another mighty passionate gal. He was sort of vexed about that, too. For chubby little Felicidad had only been pretty, while Rosalinda was downright beautiful, and built a lot more interesting, too.

He said, "We just got here. Give a man time to get used to the situation before he takes his gun rig and boots off, for Pete's sake."

She asked, "Who is this Pete, some pretty gringo boy you like more than me? I can take it that way, if that is your desire."

He stifled the laugh he felt like laughing and said, "That's an awful thing to say about the gent you call *San Pedro*, and I feel sort of insulted myself. I like gals fine, the old-fashioned way, but there's a time and a place for everything and, besides, I don't know if I can afford you. I only make a little over five hundred a year plus expenses, and I've been spending money like it was going out of style since leaving Denver."

"Oh, for why do you speak to me in such a cruel manner? Have I asked you for money, even when I risked my life for you?"

"No, and I admire gals with a romantic nature. I've always felt too romantic to pay for it, myself."

But now she had her head down on her knees and was crying fit to bust, intimating he'd called her a whore. She was a whore, but a good old gal who'd backed a dangerous play as well. He took her in his arms to soothe her and say, "Aw, mush, there's no need to carry on so silly, Rosalinda. Didn't El Gato promise all you gals would get your names engraved on stone someday? I'm sure that once Don Julio overthrows the government he'll be glad to put you in for a medal."

She didn't seem to be groping for a medal right now —Longarm was sure he hadn't hung one on his fool pecker, ever. So as she got to working on his fly buttons he said, "Hold on, now. What do you think you're doing?" even though he knew what it was.

She got it out and wailed, "I knew you loathed me! You are only half erect, you brute!"

He kissed her throat and told her, "That's more than I had any right to expect, and you're doing just fine, *querida mia.*"

So as he kissed her sweet passionate face and they both fell back across the bedding together, she got to playing with him more skillfully, and since it only seemed polite to run his free hand up under her satin skirts to return the favor, he forgot all about his earlier affair at the *posada* that same night. By now he might have gotten his second wind with old Felicidad in any case, if she hadn't insisted on leaving early, bless her consideration.

Rosalinda purred, "Oh, it's beginning to feel as if you do like me, after all. But don't you think we should get out of all these awkward clothes?"

He said that sounded like a fine idea. She beat him, easy, having less to take off, and knelt naked on the floor to haul his boot off, panting, *"Apresusa!* I am mad with passion?"

That made two of them by the time their healthy naked bodies were entwined in good clean animal lust atop the rumpled bedding. But because he'd been with another animal, earlier, Longarm took longer than usual to satisfy himself, and she took that as a compliment that satisfied her immensely.

As she moaned like a coming cougar he warned her to keep it down to at least alley cat, explaining, "I'm hot, too. But let's not forget our manners to the other guests downstairs."

She gripped him tighter around the waist with her legs and said, "Forgive me. I seldom feel free to let myself go with a man, and I have not even done this with a customer since my last indisposition of the moon.

141

Do you do this so good with all the other poor women you overpower, handsome *yanqui?*"

He said, "Only the pretty ones, and I'm not sure who might have overpowered whom, just now."

"Are you cross with me for falling for you?" she asked. He allowed he wasn't and braced himself on stiff elbows to enjoy the view of what she'd gotten him into. There was only a little light through one dusty window to see by. It was enough to see she was built nice enough to pose for one of those marble statues the Old Greeks had gone in for, although he'd never yet seen a statue posed so sassy in any museum open to the public. Since great minds ran along the same channels at such times, she gazed up at him adoringly and said, "Oh, you are so handsome and so strong and, *ay caramba,* there is so much of you!"

He stopped what he'd been doing to ask if he was hurting her. She shook her head wildly, begged him not to stop, and told him it was most considerate to show such concern.

They'd just discovered he could when the door opened enough for El Gato to say, "Oh, excuse me. I thought you might want to know your prisoner, the Great Costello, does not seem to be with us anymore."

Longarm swore, assured Rosalinda he didn't mean her. "How great a lead are we talking about," he asked El Gato, "and how come he has any at all, damn it?"

El Gato said, "The girl I sent to bed with him was watching. That is, she was until he knocked her out at a very rude as well as unexpected time. She just came to. She has no idea how long she may have been unconscious. But of course none of us have been here a full hour, you fast worker."

Longarm began to haul on his duds as he growled, "He has to be headed for the horses, risky as that may be. I thought you told me a couple of patriotic pimps were keeping an eye on things down below."

"They have been. Your prisoner did not leave by any of the usual exits. You'll never guess how he got out of a room very similar to this one."

Longarm said, "Sure I will. It occurred to me right off that if we got trapped up here my best bet would be straight up through them tiles and across the other roof-tops."

He strapped on his gun without bothering to button his vest. Rosalinda was welcome to his long johns if she had any use for them. He reached for his hat, found the gal's bare rump in the way, and patted it fondly as he said, "I'll never forget you and please hand me my hat, *querida*. I'm sorry, too, but I got to get going."

As the girl passed his Mexican sombrero to him with a sad sigh, El Gato told him, "Wait, you are not think-ing. That stable is right across from the bullring."

"Yeah," Longarm said, "but the boys we detailed to draw the whole town over that way are long gone by now and Costello knows it."

"Not all the people attracted by the false alarm, and certainly not all the local lawmen. Even if he makes it to the horses, how far can he get? He's a gringo, without a dozen words of Spanish. They'll have roadblocks set up all around the city."

Longarm said, "Yeah, but not looking for him. The Great Costello ain't wanted on any charges in Mexico, right?"

"Wrong. They know Don Julio has many *yanqui* friends. By now they have to know he never got away from them without any help. If they grab a strange gringo on the trail, and he does not know how to answer them, well . . . *los rurales* are hardly famous for their saintly patience, even with people who can talk to them."

"He rode down with us. He's heard all you just now said. You may have noticed he knows how to move sneaky, a cut above your average border jumper."

As Longarm rose from the mat, stooping some, El Gato said, "In that case I shall go with you."

"Don't you dare," Longarm protested. "I never hung by one hand off the side of a six-story building just to see Don Julio caught again. You got to get him out of here to another hideout. Fast. Don't tell me where. I don't want to know. They might catch me as well as Costello. He could be spilling the beans this very minute. So this is it and you're on your own, pard. I done all I can for you and now it's time I got back to my own chores."

El Gato and Rosalinda wished him *via con Dios* as he ducked out the door, knowing he'd need some help from the Lord. He sure wasn't getting much cooperation from anyone else.

He made it down the back stairs without incident, meaning the sneaky little son of a bitch hadn't been picked up yet. As Longarm made his way out to the front street, he knew Costello would have done the same. Whether their big hats and charro jackets worked or not in dim light, neither would have been able to thread all the way to the *posada* via the inky back alleyways of a strange town without getting hopelessly lost.

The streets of downtown Juarez weren't as crowded now, cuss all sleepy heads, but they weren't yet deserted enough for even a taller-than-usual-looking *vaquero* to draw much interest. As he got closer to the bullring a shabby young gal popped out of a doorway to ask if he was lonely. When he said he wasn't, in as good a Mexican accent as he could manage, she cursed him and said her baby brother was available, but didn't follow him.

He didn't think it would be a good notion to stroll into the *posada* by way of the front door. He was close enough, now, to work his way around to the back without getting lost. As he stood there in the darkness, trying to figure a way into the stable, a back door opened and a familiar plump figure splashed his boots with the

144

contents of a wash basin before she spotted him and sucked in her breath. Before she could let it out with a scream he moved closer and assured her, "It's me, Felicidad. Has anyone else been by, asking about us?"

She made the sign of the cross with her free hand and told him, "Not you by name, *querido*. But a short time ago *la policia* and some *rurales* lined us all up out front and made us tell them the stories of our lives. They took a man away who had no papers."

Longarm groaned and asked, "The short club-footed hombre who was here, earlier, with El Gato and me?"

"No. He was just here, for to get his horse. Didn't you know that?"

He muttered, "I do now. El Gato was right, he's acting dumb as hell. Can you sneak me into the stable from back here, Felicidad?"

She could and did. They encountered no one as she led him through the kitchen and showed him a side door into the stable.

There was nobody there but the horses. He struck a match and commenced to cuss a blue streak. When the plump *mestiza* cowered away and asked him why he was so angry, he told her, "It ain't you. It's him. The dirty little polecat took the fine army mount I was riding and left me ten dollars worth of crowbait. He's even ridden off with my possibles, Winchester, private saddle, and my favorite hat and coat!"

She suggested, "Can you not catch up with him riding El Gato's big black *caballo?*"

"Don't tempt me. El Gato may need to do some serious riding before long, and a man who'd stick a pal with a poor mount would lick up spit. That's what I mean to make the Great Costello do when I catch up with him. I might not let him lick up anything as nice as my spit, neither."

He led the livery nag from its stall and began to saddle it with the borrowed saddle that was no doubt

145

worth more. Felicidad said, "If you ride out, now, you are sure to run into a roadblock. I heard *los rurales* talking about that. Why don't you spend the rest of the night with me? I have finished all of my work and this time I will not have to ask you to stop, eh?"

He told her she had no idea how tempting her suggestion was, kissed her, and led the uglier critter out front to mount up and ride. Behind him, Felicidad wailed that he was surely going to get himself killed. He hoped she was wrong, but what she said made a lot of sense.

Chapter 17

The best way to avoid roadblocks was by avoiding roads. There was no moon, and the stars, while bright as stars could get away from city lights, didn't light up the cross-country brush and cactus worth mention. Longarm's only consolation was that it hardly seemed likely anyone could see him at any distance when he couldn't see as far as his mount's ears without squinting. He knew there were no serious cliffs between them and the Rio Bravo, and horses were said to see their way in the dark a lot better than humans. He found out how cat-eyed the old stable plug was when he hooked a tweed-clad knee on cholla, and missed his long johns considerable.

He swore, reined in, and scraped the cactus pads off with his knife, muttering, "I ought to be carrying you, you bat-blind waste of your mother's oats." But he would have found it even harder to find his way north on foot, of course. So he heeled the nag into further slow but steady progress, saying, "Pay attention, damn it."

Since Juarez was a border town, the border wasn't far enough to matter. As he walked his mount slowly, which was about all it could manage, Longarm kept an ear cocked for the sound of running water and an eye peeled for night fires. He was hoping bored border guards would be considerate enough to light one, once they'd been stuck long enough in one place to feel how cold the desert night could get this close to sunrise.

He failed to see anything but stars above a dull, black blanket of nothingness. One place was as good as another to cross the river, this far east of the more sensible as well as official ford between Juarez and El Paso. He figured by this time the Great Costello would have made it across, if he hadn't drowned or been picked up. Neither Mexicans nor Americans were dumb enough to plant street lamps near a river that couldn't make up its mind whether it was Cherry Creek or the wide Missouri from time to time. But now he could see pinpoints of light off to the north-west. They told him he was maybe three or four miles east of El Paso, and just south of Fort Bliss, if they hadn't moved it. He didn't think the Great Costello would want to aim for the military post, as his best chance would be a beeline for downtown El Paso and another hole-up with his gang. Once he was out of sight with that clubbed foot, the game would start from scratch with a fresh deck.

He forged on for the river. Then he heard the hammer of a repeating rifle click in front of him and, worse yet, someone levered a round behind as a sinister voice between him and the country of his birth asked, *"Quien es?"*

Seeing this was no time to be taken for smart, Longarm called back in English, "Howdy. I am U.S. Deputy Marshal Long, on the trail of an Anglo outlaw. I don't

148

suppose you boys have seen a runty rascal on a handsome chestnut gelding?"

His unseen questioner switched to bad English and replied, "We heard someone crossing the river just now. He did not seem fit for to stop when I yelled halt. We were about to cross over and see where he might have fallen. You, of course, are under arrest and, if you try anything funny, you shall die right here, slowly."

Another voice called out, "*Sí*, is fun for to gut-shoot you gringos. You do not know for how to die with dignity."

Longarm said, "I can see you boys have to be *rurales*. Before you gut-shoot anybody, you'd best listen tight. For despite your surly manners I'm a friendly cuss, and I just might be able to save your asses for you."

Their leader moved close enough to Longarm to make him out as a blur, albeit his sergeant's stripes weren't visible as he sort of purred, "I am a sweetheart, too, except when you suckers of pigs' corkscrew cocks are around. Say something friendly, gringo."

"Don Julio Valdez got away clean," Longarm said. "You're never going to catch him, now."

There was a moment of ominous silence before the *rurale* leader opined, "That did not sound so friendly. How do you know about the escape of that political prisoner, gringo?"

"A little pussy cat I know told me. Before you get your bowels in an uproar, I don't know where El Gato and old Valdez might be right now. So tying me down atop an ant pile would be a waste of time and you boys don't have much time."

"We are still listening, gringo. So are the ants."

"Shit, nothing you can do to me will smart as much as what *El Presidente*'s professional torturers are going to do to you, if you ever fall into their hands after letting Valdez get away. You know you don't know how he

149

done it, and I know you don't know how he done it, but before old Diaz is convinced, you're all going to suffer considerable."

The *rurale* sergeant purred, "You won't be there to see it whether they catch us or not."

"We're running out of dark as well as time. It's got to be after four in the morning and none of us want to be on this side of the border when the sun pops up. So cut the gringo-baiting, listen tight, and I'll tell you what you'd best do."

"*You* are going to tell *us?*" their sergeant roared as all the others laughed. The laughing men added up to more than a dozen.

Longarm said, "Damned if the skyline ain't visible over to the east, now. You boys could gun me for my boots or the hell of it, and likely make it across the river before it's broad-ass day. But then where would you go in them big *rurale* hats? Even the Anglos are sore at you in El Paso and, if army patrols from Fort Bliss ain't patting down every cactus for miles for hidden weapons, their post commander has neither imagination nor ambition worth mention."

"Bah, I spit in his mother's milk. We are neither Apache nor mere bandits. We know a thing or two about such matters."

"I ain't finished and I'm glad you've done such tracking your ownselves. It saves having to explain the odds in detail. Suffice it to say you're talking about hiding out a large party of new faces under big hats, with no visible means of support, on range they've never rode before. Any Tex-Mex you meet is likely to shoot first and ask about them *rurale* uniforms later. I doubt many an Anglo-Tex would ask questions before or after, and since it was your own government who had the great notion about Indian scalps being cash redeemable, we'd best not even talk about you boys meeting up with Apache if you make for less populated parts."

150

The *rurale* sergeant shrugged and said, "You have made your point. We shall have to keep our wits about us until we get some money and gringo hats. But we are used to getting what we want."

"I can still show you how to avoid your perhaps just desserts from Mexico without taking on the U.S. and Texas combined. But why don't we talk about it on the far side of the river? Yonder horizon is pearling by the minute and I can already see the tops of fourteen big gray hats at this range."

The *rurale* sergeant seemed to think that was a sensible notion and so they were soon all mounted up and fording the Rio Bravo in a bunch, with Longarm in the middle. A couple of them made rude remarks about him in Spanish. He didn't let on as if he understood. So they got to talking more freely in their own lingo, and it was good to hear they didn't plan on shooting him down like a dog until he'd gotten them someplace safer.

By the time they'd ridden a few miles north he could see the features of the *rurale* sergeant riding to his right. The Mex was larded over some from self-indulgence, but big and mean as one had to be to ride for such a mean outfit. As the rising sun gilded the tips of the mesquite and cactus all around, he asked Longarm just where they might be headed. So Longarm said, "Fort Bliss. You'll like it. The starting pay for a U.S. Cavalry trooper is thirteen dollars a month and all the beans he can eat. How much do they pay you *rurales* in peso paper?"

"They expect us to pick up a little extra on the side. But you can't be serious, you just said your army is out looking for us!"

Longarm nodded and said, "I did. I doubt they'll be expecting you to ride in for breakfast. With me vouching for you, I can promise you breakfast at least. Whether they're willing to take you in entire or not will be up to them, of course."

151

The sergeant laughed like hell, turned in his saddle, and called out, "This crazy *cabrón* wants us to join the *Americano* army!" and while some laughed, at least a couple opined it sounded safer, if not easier, than joining the Apache nation.

The sergeant turned back to Longarm and repeated that he was crazy, adding, "Who ever heard of anyone but *yanquis* joining the *yanqui* army?"

"Me. More than half of the enlisted men are immigrants. Most of the native-born who join are colored. I never said it was considered a good job. A man can make a lot more as a cowhand, if he don't mind working hard."

The larded-over sergeant rode on in silence for a time before he growled, "Tell me, how difficult do you think it would be for a man with my military experience to make a few stripes in your own army?"

Longarm laughed and said, "There you go. Bucking for corporal before you've spent an hour in the chow line. To be honest with such an honest cuss, I can't rightly say how long it takes to get promoted in a peacetime army. I met an old German boy, up near the South Pass during the Shoshone rising, who'd made buck sergeant in one hitch. Of course, he'd been an officer in the Prussian army, before he got in trouble with his colonel's wife and had to join another army, fast, as a private. His English wasn't as good as yours. On the other hand, he'd likely had more experience, fighting the French and all."

The *rurale* sergeant snapped, "That's a lie. I fought the French Legion at Camerone when we rose against Louis Napoleon's puppet emperor, Maximillian. I guess I am as good a soldier as any square-headed *alemán!*"

Longarm didn't answer. The sky above was clear as well as blue, now. The early morning air was cool, but it looked as if they were in for another scorcher. He still wanted his frock coat and more regular hat back, damn it.

One of the others called out in Spanish, asking their leader where on earth they were riding so boldly in broad daylight. The sergeant called back, "This one says we should join the *Americano* army. Don't laugh. It's beginning to make sense to me. It's the last place anyone they send after us would look for us. It avoids a lot of tedious discussion with the Texas Rangers as well, and, what the devil, if we don't like it we can always ride on, with fresh mounts as well as gringo disguises."

They thought that was funny as hell. They were still joshing back and forth, promoting each other to lance corporal or putting each other on kitchen police when, ahead in the distance, a bugle blew and a tiny flag rose above the chaparral. Longarm said, "I figured it was morning. It's more gloomy in the winter, when they run the colors up in the dark. The army pays no mind to the weather outside. Are you boys still with me?"

The *rurale* sergeant hesitated. Then he said, "Why not? You were all too right about every other hand being turned against us now. But what if they don't need new recruits?"

"Oh, I feel sure they'll take you in. They got recruiting stands set up on the docks to grab greenhorns getting off the boats. Thirteen dollars sounds like more to a Swede than say a farmboy from Iowa."

It must have sounded like a lot to a Mexican as well. The *rurale* leader said, *"Bueno.* But how are we to explain these uniforms we already have on?"

"Let me do the talking. I know the officers and it ain't like deserting from foreign outfits is a federal offense in the U.S. of A. I told you about that German boy who had to leave the Prussian army sort of informal."

And so, while some in the rear ranks still voiced a few reservations, Longarm was soon leading the ragged column of gray-clad *rurales* across the parade of Fort Bliss toward the guardhouse. From the barracks all around, blue-clad troopers gaped, and officers who'd meant to sleep a mite longer woke up.

Longarm reined in near the guardhouse and dismounted first as a wary-eyed sergeant of the guard came out to ask him what was going on. He murmured, "We got a dawn patrol out searching for Mex border raiders, Longarm. I sure hope you can vouch for this bunch."

Longarm said, "I figured you might be on the prod out here, that's how come I had 'em ride in, slow, across the parade. Did I give you time to rouse the supernumerary gun hands inside?"

The army man said, "You did, and the officer of the day ought to be headed this way by now as well."

Longarm nodded, turned on his heel, and called out to the still-mounted *rurales*, "You boys are all under arrest on the charge of crossing the border uninvited, more than once."

The *rurale* sergeant gasped and roared, *"Traidor!* You told us you would help us join your army!"

"You weren't listening sharp. I only said I felt sure they'd take you in. So I took you in to 'em and—"

Then he had to shoot the *rurale* sergeant out of his saddle because the cuss was slapping leather. He only got one other *rurale* as the rest lit out in all directions, calling him and the U.S. Army awful names.

But, of course, none of them got all that far with the guard detail blazing away with rifles, and more than one pistol firing from windows all around as the confused *rurales* milled in dusty confusion until every saddle was empty.

By the time the last shots echoed away and the dust was starting to settle, the officer of the day was coming with the corporal of the guard at his left. They both had their service revolvers out. As they joined Longarm and the sergeant of the guard, the O.D. stared soberly out across the carnage and put his gun away, saying, "My, what a pleasant surprise. How did you do that, Longarm?"

The tall deputy smiled modestly and said, "I had to. They was planning to murder me as soon as I guided 'em to safety. So I figured this was the safest place for me to guide 'em. I didn't want such disgusting gents running loose in the U.S. of A. in any case. But now I got to get going, Lieutenant. This unplanned side trip has given more important killers I'm after one hell of a lead on me."

The O.D. said, "We were afraid they'd killed you, too, when the army mount we loaned you came home without you."

Longarm blinked and asked, "My saddle, gear, and that chestnut wound up here, you say?"

The O.D. nodded and said, "We were just talking about it, over at the corrals, when you showed up as well. The gelding came in lathered and jaded, as if you'd really put him through some hard riding."

Longarm said, "I didn't do it all to the poor brute. The Great Costello swapped mounts with me down Mexico way and no doubt rode like the devil was after him, even if it was only me. I was expecting to catch up with my hat and all in El Paso, not out here, though."

The O.D. shrugged and said, "Maybe the chestnut threw a rider who abused him and just naturally decided to come on home."

Longarm thought before he sighed and said, "That would be too nice to ask. The little bastard is a fair rider, even on a poor mount. Try her this way. He made her to El Paso, or close enough to matter. Then he turned the chestnut loose, knowing it was an army mount who'd be likely to rejoin the army. He had no way of knowing I was headed here instead of into town after him. He done it to throw me off his trail. I was supposed to scout every livery and hitching post in El

Paso in vain while he and his sidekicks made further plans. But, thanks to them good old boys sprawled all about us, I don't have to waste as much time as he counted on, searching for my stuff. I got a railroad timetable in my frock coat, too, if it's still rolled in my possibles. I'd best go see."

As he headed for the corrals, the O.D. ordered the sergeant of the guard to do something about all those bodies before the colonel's lady saw them and had a fit. Then he chased after Longarm, caught up, and said, "We'll have to issue you a fresh mount if you're going after them again. What was that about a timetable?"

Longarm said, "I can get me and both saddles back to town aboard the livery nag I have to return in any case. That magic act gone bad won't be planning on riding out on horseback. They know he'd attract less attention aboard a train, and I think there's an eastbound express coming through this side of noon."

Chapter 18

The timetable Longarm found in his recovered coat confirmed his thoughts. The eastbound flier was due to stop for water and whatever in El Paso at ten-fifty-five, pull out at eleven, and not stop until it had another drink at the Pecos.

Longarm had plenty of time to get into town, even aboard the overloaded stable nag. But he suspected they'd have members of the magicians guild watching for him and, worse yet, he had no idea where they were holed up in downtown El Paso. So he didn't go there.

He rode into Mex Town, short of his goal, and when he reined in by a *herrería* and told the Mex blacksmith he was a friend of El Gato, they said they'd be proud to guard both saddles and the tired old nag to the death.

He took advantage of their hospitality to put on a more sensible hat, and gave the charro jacket to a grinning kid who looked like he'd always wanted one. Then he walked on, in shirt sleeves and vest, with the Win-

chester from his McClellen cradled in one elbow, and
his .44-40 still riding his left hip, cross-draw.

Since Mex Town lay on the less fashionable side of
the tracks, Longarm saw no need to approach the depot
via its front entrance, and legged it across the yards
from the south. Nobody challenged him but a big desert
locust buzzing atop a rail, as if it thought he'd take it for
a rattlesnake. When he didn't, it flew off on its under-
sized butterfly wings and cussed him some more from a
safer distance. He'd forecasted the weather right for a
change. The sun was glaring down with hellish glee and
it wasn't near noon yet.

He climbed up on the deserted sunbaked loading
platform and entered the depot from the less expected
side. The waiting room was empty. The blackboard
above the ticket window agreed with his printed timetable. He went over to the window and asked the white-
haired and bearded gent behind the brass bars if he'd
sold a mess of railroad tickets in recent memory. The
old-timer didn't bother to look up as he muttered, "I just
came on duty. You're the first customer I've had so far."

Longarm said, "I ain't a customer, I'm the law. I'm
hunting a sort of vaudeville troupe, in a hurry to move
on. I figure, let's see, half a dozen gals and four men
left."

The old-timer on the far side of the bars shook his
white head and said, "Ain't seen even one good-looking
gal so far today."

Longarm hauled out his watch and muttered, "Damn,
it's even later than I figured. If someone was in too
great a hurry to buy tickets from you, they could just get
on and work it out with the conductor, though, right?"

The old-timer shrugged and said, "Sure. Why not?"

Longarm put his watch away, saying, "Well, for one
thing it's not the way I'd do it if I wanted to travel
without attracting much attention. If I was a bunch, I
reckon I'd get on sort of separate, with tickets in all my

158

hands, and sort of sit spread out like I didn't know me at all."

The old goat in the ticket booth didn't have any suggestions to offer about that. Longarm thanked him and made his way over to the front entrance. The sunbaked street out front was empty, save for a dust devil swirling up the sunny side like an officious ghost. Everyone at this hour would be at work, until lunch time at least. Morning deliveries had all been made and nobody with a lick of sense brought fresh produce into town under a Texican summer sun.

So how come three distant figures were coming down the center of the street from the north, as if they'd never heard of shade?

Longarm stepped out under the depot's overhang to study them as they came toward him. The one in the middle was short, wearing a big Mex sombrero and charro jacket. The gun rig he had strapped on looked less familiar. He was walking, with a slight limp, between a matching pair of female travel dusters and, though they both had sunbonnets on, the red hair down to their shoulders matched, too. He couldn't tell, yet, if they were true identical twins, or just close enough to look the same at any distance. Longarm waited until all three of them were about a hundred feet away, midway between either shaded walk, before he stepped out into the sunlight and called out, "Howdy. I see you still have someone watching my hotel and stable. But, as you see, there's more than one way to get to El Paso, and I fear you won't be leaving it as planned, neither."

The two more feminine figures moved away to either side as their old man gave them stage cues Longarm couldn't make out. He let that go, for now. Gunning women was considered sort of sissy, and the Great Costello had said all the killing had been done by the male members of his troupe.

Longarm called out, "You're doing fine, so far. Now

159

I'd like you to unbuckle that gun rig, slow and polite, and let that hog leg fall anywhere it has a mind to."

The other man didn't seem to admire that notion. He called back, in an oddly strangled tone, "Damn it, we made a deal!"

Longarm shook his head and said, "This wasn't it, Costello. I might have gone along with your loco notion, south of the border where U.S. laws ain't binding, but you was the one who chose to pull a fast one. So all bets are off and I'm still waiting for you to unbuckle that gun."

The other man's big sombrero swung sort of comical as he shook his head and insisted, "If you had any sense of honor at all you'd put aside that Winchester and have it out with me man to man, damn it!"

Longarm snorted in mingled disgust and surprise. The only two gals in sight to comment on his honor were the sunbonnet twins, now well clear of his field of fire to either side of the street. But then a window opened across the way and another gal stuck her head out to see what all the fussing was about.

Longarm called back, "It's as tempting to let you have it your own dumb way than to simply gun you if you won't do as I say. So how about it, Costello? Are you willing to come quiet or do I have to take you noisy?"

The lonely little figure took a step backwards but didn't look any more cooperative as he jeered, "I dare you, big man. What's the matter, are you afraid of me?"

Longarm swore softly in disbelief. Then he hunkered to lean his Winchester against the steps, straightened up with a puzzled but determined smile, and stalked forward, growling, "All right, if that's the way you want it."

Then, as his intended target kept the range between them the same distance by crawfishing backward up the center of the street, Longarm added, "Aw, for Pete's sake, make up your mind, Costello. If you don't want to

160

fight, just do as I say. If you want to fight, slap leather, damn it. It's too hot to chase you. I didn't even want to fight you, damn it. It was your notion to hold this fool duel. So hold still and let's get to it."

It didn't work. His quarry didn't seem to want to draw any more than he wanted to stop walking backwards. Longarm was almost abreast of the gals to either side, now. That was how far the fool had backed. Longarm called out, "This foolishness has gone far enough, Costello. I'm going to count to three. If you've neither gone for that gun or raised you hands by that time I'm fixing to go for mine, and end it, one way or another, hear?"

The sort of pathetic little gent didn't seem to be paying any heed as Longarm started counting. Longarm already wished he'd said he'd draw on the count of ten. It was too one-sided. The poor little rascal didn't have a chance.

Or did he?

Longarm swore and dropped to one knee as one of the innocent-looking redheads put a .32 slug through the space he'd been about to step into. He fired back, sending the duster-clad sweet miss crashing back through the window of a feed store, and then he'd spun his knee to fire at the other as, sure enough, she seemed to be aiming at him, too!

That inspired the more masculine figure who'd been crawfishing him into the cross fire of the twins to go for his own gun at last. Since Longarm already had his own out, it was a poor move indeed.

As his target tossed that sombrero high as only a spine-shot gent could manage with just his head, a bullet tore dust a lot closer to Longarm, and went screaming off into the distance with a harmless banshee wail. Longarm leaped up, pegged a shot into the smoke cloud near the door of the depot behind him, and took a running dive over a watering trough to enjoy some shade, a place to reload, and a chance to sort out his thoughts.

By the time he had it figured out, police whistles were blowing and the street wasn't empty anymore. Longarm rose from his hiding hole and moved out to join the gents standing over the one he'd downed in the center of the street. One of them wearing a copper badge, recognized Longarm, took in the .44-40 he was still holding, albeit pointed politely down, and asked him, "Did you do this and who was he, Longarm?"

Longarm had already guessed, from the exposed brown hair, that he might not have shot the Great Costello after all. He rolled the body on its back with his boot, stared soberly down, and said, "He was eating dinner at my hotel the same time I was last evening. I reckon he was keeping an eye on more than his steak and spuds. That accounts for one more male member of the bunch as robbed your post office. I was supposed to take him for their leader."

Another more excited gent ran up to them, complaining, "I just had a redheaded gal in a travel duster delivered through my front window. Only, when we looked closer, it was a man with a red wig and gal's duster over his more natural duds."

Longarm said, "That's two we don't have to worry about, then. I was mighty worried about a real female redhead I know. But when someone's shooting at you, gallantry can get you killed. I think I left another one under yonder awning. Let's go see if it was a him or a her."

It was a him, once they got the sunbonnet and red wig off. Longarm sighed with relief and said, "I saw him escorting a real redhead to the depot last night. He must have been the one who told the Great Costello she left with me instead of a train. So that still leaves the Great Costello. And if that ain't a train whistle I hear in the distance right now some lobo wolf has sure picked an odd hour to howl at the moon."

He headed back to the depot at a run, with the town law and some just plain helpful El Paso gents in tow. He scooped up his Winchester, entered the waiting room, and saw it was empty. You could still smell gunsmoke, though.

He moved over to the ticket window. Before he could ask, the white-haired cuss in the booth said, "They run out to the platform. A short man and a taller redheaded gal. Who was they shooting at, just now?"

Longarm didn't answer. He was already streaking for the platform exit. He skidded to a stop on the dry, splintered planks to stare far and wide across the dusty yards. Everything was moving. Heat waves made 'em move on a day like today. But he saw nothing worth chasing, at first. Then he spotted a distant but rapidly growing column of black smoke.

As one of the town lawmen joined him to ask, "See anything?" Longarm said, "Yeah. The train they mean to board is coming in. Would you stay out here and let me know if you see anybody popping out of thin air to board it? I got to talk some more to that old ticket clerk."

The town lawman agreed. Longarm went back inside, moved over to the brass-barred window, and said, "You forgot to mention they had wings. How many tickets did you sell them before they lit out?"

The white-bearded gent behind the bars replied, "Six, as a matter of fact. That was before the gent with the gal started blazing away out yon doorway, of course. How was I to know they was homicidal lunatics? I just work here."

Longarm grinned wolfishly and said, "No you don't. It was a nice try, Costello. But now I want you to put both hands on the counter and just keep them there

163

whilst this nice El Paso lawman here kicks his way in to disarm you."

The white-wigged and fake-bearded rogue on the far side of the brass bars did no such thing. As he crabbed sideways out of sight Longarm shouted "Down!" but did some crabbing on his own instead. When the Great Costello fired through the planking between them, Longarm wasn't directly in the line of fire and only picked up some splinters with his pants.

He fired back with his Winchester, of course, and his own calculations worked better, judging by the awful yelp and dull thud inside the ticket booth. He fired some more in the direction of the thud and heard Costello cry out, "I give! I give!" He ceased fire as he moved down to the door and kicked it in, or tried to. Something soft and soggy was blocking further progress at floor level.

Longarm put his back into it and shoved the door open wider by sort of sliding the body of the real ticket clerk on the lubrication of his own blood. Then he stepped in and threw down on the other man at the far end of the narrow booth. The Great Costello was half reclined and half sitting up, with his shoulders wedged in a corner. He'd lost his white theatrical wig, and his fake beard was flecked with blood as well as sort of loose. As the treacherous clubfoot coughed again Longarm asked, in a conversational tone, "Couldn't you have just bound and gagged this other gent, you murderous little shit?"

"He put up a struggle," explained the Great Costello, as if it justified cutting a man's throat like that. The flooring under all of them rumbled as, outside, the east-bound flier rolled into the station. Longarm knew the others, outside, could take care of such explaining as might be needed. He moved closer to the man he'd downed, hunkered down beside him, and after sliding Costello's Remington .45 clear, patted Costello down, found a .32 Harrington Richardson whore pistol in a vest pocket, and said, "Shame on you. It's my considered medical opinion that you don't need a doc. But as long as you can still talk, could we discuss some of your recent waywardness in hopes of clearing a few minor details up?"

The great Costello grimaced and asked, "Why? I don't owe you shit. You just treated me and my poor relations mean as hell."

"It was your notion to let them take all those chances," Longarm said. "I noticed down Mexico way that while you liked to plan razzle-dazzles, it was El Gato and me you expected to take the real risk. You told your nephews or whatever about the dueling brag you'd made, then got them to play you and two gals I'd be even less likely to shoot at. All four of you were hoping I wouldn't get here before that train outside. But just in case I did, you set it up with the dice loaded in your own favor."

The dying man coughed and grumbled, "How were we to know you were immortal, for God's sake? How did you see through my neat disguise, Longarm?"

The younger and smarter man in the booth replied, "I didn't, at first, even though I ought to be stood in the corner for being so dumb. It only occurred to me, after you'd made one last dumb move, that you'd said you just came on duty, in the middle of the morning. When I show up for work around ten I get pure hell at my office. But, like you counted on, nobody pays all that much attention to ticket clerks. So how was I to know you'd come in ahead of your act to act as a lookout and make sure all of you could board that train with tickets, cheap, and no record of the transaction or probable destination?"

"You're wrong," Costello said, "I do need a doctor. It's starting to hurt, now that the shock's wearing off."

Longarm soothed, "Try to breathe shallow. Let your lungs fill up with blood natural and it won't hurt so bad.

Where are the gals, Costello? I know you was trying to send Maureen on ahead when we made our little deal. Where were you all planning to meet up again, later?"

"Go to hell. They got away clean. I give you my word none of them had any hand in the jobs the boys and I pulled off while they kept the home fire burning."

"No offense, but your word ain't much. I reckon it was fair for you to give me the slip down Mexico way after all that empty boasting about a fair man-to-man showdown. I didn't mind fibbing to some *rurales* who meant to double-cross me in the end. But the boys I just shot it out with were your kin. You told 'em they only had to play their parts and that if I was really here before that train you'd do the real fighting behind my misdirected back. The one playing you must have liked to shit his pants when I kept coming and you took so long getting up the nerve to back-shoot me. You had me in a four-way cross fire and you blew it. Pearl of Wisdom told me your magic act was marred by a bad sense of timing. Like a lot of half-ass magicians, you knew all the tricks, but your stage fright made you hesitant and clumsy."

The Great Costello closed his eyes, gave a sad little moan, and went limp. Longarm reached with his free hand to feel for a pulse. The magician's small, strong hand suddenly clamped on his wrist and he said, "Gotcha!" Then he laughed like hell and died.

An El Paso lawman who'd eased into the booth in time to hear the last of it asked, "Is he?" and Longarm said, "He is, and in a way I'm sort of disappointed. I figured if anyone was about to escape from a situation like this, it would have to be him."

Chapter 19

Longarm had better luck on the train back to Denver than he'd had coming down. Her name was Susan and she said she sold female notions, wholesale, and that while she was on her way to Denver to practice her traveling trade she didn't know a soul in town. So after he'd bought her some sickening cocktails in the club car and persuaded her to try tequila *mucho gusto* cocktails instead, it seemed only natural for her to invite him to her compartment and show him her line of wares.

He had no use for black silk stockings or the lacey garters ladies used to hold 'em up with. Once he had old Susan out of her own black lace, he decided making love on sooty sheets wasn't all that bad, now that it wasn't so hot and sticky on the high plains.

The traveling saleswoman had hair—all over—the same color as that chestnut gelding he'd said adios to down at Fort Bliss, albeit she was built a lot more petite. She gave a man a good ride for such a diminutive mount, and by the time the train got them both to

167

Denver she was still frisky. So when she pleaded with him to meet her after working hours at her hotel near the Union Depot, she didn't have to twist his arm. Longarm did have friends in Denver, but there were still a few positions he hadn't gotten around to, yet, with old Susan.

They shook on it and parted friendly after he helped her get her sample bags over to her hotel. Then, knowing Billy Vail was as interested in railroad timetables as he was, Longarm started legging it uptown to the federal building to build some character with his boss. He didn't even stop for breakfast, even though he hadn't managed any aboard the train. This was one time he didn't want to wind up working late.

As he was crossing Larimer Street, Crawford of the *Post* grabbed him by the elbow and steered him under the awning of a vaudeville theatre on the shady side of the street. Crawford said, "We got most of it from the wire service, but I want an interview from you, anyway. Weren't you scared when you found yourself in a four-way cross fire down El Paso way?"

Longarm said, "I was scared when I only figured it was three ways. You can quote me on that. I'm only a hero, not a total asshole. Now let go of my damn buttonhole and let me get on to my damn office. Knowing Billy Vail, it's been open for hours. He has his own key and must figure they expect him to milk cows at the federal building every morning."

But the reporter was insistent. So Longarm answered a few more fool questions, tersely, as his eyes wandered over the new three-sheets posted out front by the theatre. Pearl of Wisdom was of course long gone, and he didn't recognize anyone on the new bill as an old pal who put out. He finally got loose and ducked around the corner to beeline for the office. Thanks to his meeting with old Crawford, there went the beer he'd meant to have at the Parthenon as well. He entered the federal

168

building dry, and morosely climbed the marble steps to the second floor. As he entered the Federal Marshal's layout, old Henry, the prissy young dude who played the typewriter out front, congratulated him on a job well done and said to go right on back. Longarm knew they were plotting against him.

Billy Vail didn't glance at the banjo clock on the wall this time as Longarm took a weary seat across from him. Longarm was trying to decide whether he was out of shape or whether shapely Susan lifted weights, when his boss said, "I just got a curious telegram from the Mexican government. I thought I told you to stay the hell out of Mexico."

Longarm smiled sheepishly and said, "You have my word I shot them *rurales* on our side of the border, Billy."

Vail tried not to smile as he replied, "Well, far be it from me to call anyone big as you a liar, but they do say a gringo answering to your description left one *rurale* sort of bent out of shape in a Juarez hotel. But all's well as ends well, and Don Julio was a pal of mine when I was riding with the Rangers. What are we going to do about them magical outlaws I sent you after?"

Longarm reached for a cheroot as he protested, "Hell, Billy, if you'd pay more attention to wires from me than wires from that piss-ant Diaz, you'd know all six of 'em must be planted by this time. They said, down El Paso way, it's ever a good notion to dig graves as soon as possible after a good rain, down yonder."

Vail beamed at him and said, "It ain't true that Ned Buntline writes pure bull about the wild west. You treated them rascals wild as hell. But whilst the male members of the Great Costello's traveling act have all been accounted for, the women they was traveling with ain't."

Longarm shrugged and said, "I noticed. But what the hell, none of their gals took part in any hanging offenses and, without Costello and his clan of wild Irishmen to lead 'em from the straight and narrow, they've no doubt split up and gone back to just being wild and wicked. The gents in the outfit were all related, and two of the gals were Costello's daughters, but the rest was likely stage-struck gals they picked up along the way."

"Back east, some time ago, before they went from bad to worse," Vail said. "They have neither kith nor kin out west. They don't know the parts they ain't been to before. I figure they'll stick together and backtrack along the primrose paths they know so well."

Longarm sighed and said, "Well, they ain't in El Paso, and I don't want to go up to Leadville. I got better things to do here in Denver than round up poor scared doxies the federal prosecutor down the hall has no real use for. Can't we call the case closed, for Pete's sake?"

Vail shook his head and said, "Not until it is, old son. You may have nailed all the more murderous members of the gang, but what about the money?"

Longarm lit his cheroot and said, "I wish you'd read the reports that give me writer's cramp. I told you we found around four hundred plus change in the pockets of them gents now buried in El Paso. They was carrying no luggage. With the help of El Paso P.D., I back-tracked 'em all to the various hotels they'd been holed up in. Needless to say, they hadn't left any money behind. I reckon one of Costello's twin daughters was holding on to the bulk of the loot for safekeeping. It wasn't the one called Maureen, I searched her just before she lit out of town with no luggage, either."

He took a thoughtful drag on his smoke before he nodded and said, "All right. Say they spent a good part of the loot from that first robbery, but never had time or reason to spend all the money from that post office safe in El Paso. We're talking about . . . Ouch, more money than you and me figure to draw from Uncle Sam together in the next dozen years or more. But the trail is cold, Billy. I only know what one of them gals looks like for sure, and they could have gone most anywhere by now."

Vail said, flatly, "One of 'em, at least, was here in Denver about the time you was shooting it out with her father, lover, or whatever. She cashed a couple of hundred dollars worth of stamps at the main post office a spit and a holler from this very office. Ain't that a bitch?"

Longarm scowled and said, "It was dumb as hell, too. They just couldn't have spent all that cash they stole already."

Then he blew a thoughtful smoke ring and studied it as he mused on, "Wait a second. It works if only one of the gals was packing most of the cash and a sister in sin run low on funds before they could all meet up again. I hope the post office gave some thought to what the gal cashing all them stamps might have looked like?"

Vail nodded and said, "They did. They saw no call to grab her until a supervisor recalled the flier on them special delivery stamps, too late. But the clerk who made the awful mistake says them stamps was redeemed by a mighty pretty redhead. How do you like them apples?"

Longarm whistled and said, "Unless they get a buy on henna rinse it don't make sense. Costello might have entrusted one of his twin daughters with the proceeds of that last robbery, but I suspicion one of the other men grabbed them sheets of stamps as icing on the cake for his own lady love."

"Whoever she was," Vail said, "even a hundred dollars is enough to rent them a house or fancy French flat for two or three months. She'd have never risked cashing that many stamps if all she'd planned on was a fancy dinner and a Pullman berth east. So it adds up to them meeting somewhere here in Denver, dividing up the loot, and leaving town together or separate by, say, election time, when anyone who wasn't as smart as you and me should have given up on 'em, see?"

Longarm blew another smoke ring and said, "You surely are a poor loser, boss. What am I supposed to do now, canvas every real estate agent and beauty shop in town?"

"Nope. I got lesser lights doing that already, and since Denver P.D. wants in on the case, they're searching for a gaggle of good-looking wild geese as well. I was hoping you'd be able to come up with one of your more clever notions. So why don't you?"

Longarm shrugged and said, "Well, since the twins leading the female fugitives was brung up in the magical trade, they'll no doubt make some sneaky moves above and beyond the usual fugitives. Can I borrow Smiley, Dutch, and Guilfoyle this evening? Like me, old Guilfoyle has reasons for not being the arresting officer in the case of one such gal. But I reckon we can work it out so nobody has to arrest anyone he screwed, when the time comes."

Chapter 20

It was a weeknight, so even the Denver Dry Goods & Department store was closed by sundown. When he met Susan in the lobby of her hotel, she said they already had her line of goods in stock at Denver Dry Goods, but that she'd made a few modest sales and was looking forward to an evening of less walking and more healthy exercise.

As he carried her sample bag upstairs for her Longarm said, "Well, there went a great notion I had about a dance hall up on Colfax. But what say, after we have supper, we take in a vaudville act on Larimer?"

She unlocked her door and stepped in ahead of him, protesting, "I don't want to see any damned dancing poodle dogs or listen to any damned trained seals play music, Custis. Take off your duds and let me entertain us both, right."

He case a wistful eye on the big bed in the one small room and told her, "It's early. We got to eat if you expect me to survive another night with you."

She stopped unpinning her hat and turned back to him to say, "All right. There's a dining room right downstairs. Guess what I mean to serve you for dessert."

He didn't argue, yet. He waited until they were seated in the dining room and she was sipping her *mucho gusto* before he told her, "I hope you won't get sore enough to bust plates over my head, honey, but as I told you when we first met, I ride for the Justice Department."

She smiled wickedly across the table at him and said, "They sure taught you a lot about riding, dear. But didn't you say you'd be off duty by the time I finished for the day?"

"I did, but my boss is an infernal spoilsport. He asked me to check something out for him this evening and I reckon I have to, unless we want him pounding on your door just as we're starting to enjoy ourselves."

Susan didn't answer as the waiter came over to take their order. He was one of those snooty-looking hotel waiters who acted like a ration of *chili con carne* over a T-bone was an unusual order. He seemed to think Susan's notion of trout and string beans was more civilized. When he'd left she asked Longarm what Billy Vail wanted him to do on her time, damn it.

He said, "Maybe nothing. Remember me telling you about them wicked young gals who got away whilst I was tracking down their men-folk? I don't recall if I told you they was vaudeville entertainers or not."

"You did, while we were getting our second wind. Is that why you just invited me to watch a vaudeville show with you, for heaven's sake?"

"You don't have to come along if you got better things to do," he said. "I figured to sort of combine business with pleasure by inviting you along. There's only a bare outside chance I've guessed right, and there won't be no danger, either way. If I picked the wrong three-sheets, we'll be able to leave early and be back

174

upstairs in no time. If my wild hunch pays off, it won't take more than an hour or so to book the wicked gals. So how's about it?"

She hesitated. Then she said, "Well, I wouldn't want you to think I'm a poor sport, and it does sound sort of exciting. Who told you those bad girls might be at that theatre this evening?"

He smiled modestly and said, "Me. Knowing the bills had just changed yesterday, I took a noonday walk the length of Larimer and read all the three-sheets. You was right about poodle dogs and trained seals. Slapstick comics and jugglers seem to be in oversupply this season as well. But there was only one place with a magic act on the bill. There was no matinee this afternoon, so I had to take the doorman's word that none of the gals in the all-gal act are redheads. You got to admit, though, that an all-gal act is sort of unusual."

The waiter brought their order, sniffed at Longarm, and left them alone some more. Susan said, "Oh, dear, I'm afraid I'll have to sit through small-time vaudeville in vain. You told me you only knew what one of those girls you're after really looks like. Wouldn't she be terribly stupid to show her red mop in the same town you patrol, dear?"

He frowned and said, "I don't patrol Denver, they got boys in blue to do that. I said it was a long shot. There's no law against putting on all-gal magic acts. On the other hand, a mess of strange gals boarding in town with no visible means of support could attract more attention than they want to attract and, since magic acting is the only honest profession they have—"

"I said I'd tag along," Susan cut in with a sigh. "I certainly hope you'll be as good a sport, later. For there's something I read in a wicked book that I've always been sort of curious about. I've been waiting for a good sport who doesn't seem easy to shock before I got around to really trying it."

175

Chapter 21

"This is really dreadful," Susan was saying from the vantage point of their private box as she and Longarm watched a couple of men in baggy pants slap each other with slapsticks. Longarm had been able to spring for such luxury because his office would be paying for it. A box seat cost more than it was worth, even in such a second-rate house. At least half the audience below them needed a bath and the rest were smoking tobacco worse than old Billy Vail admired.

Longarm glanced down at his printed program and soothed, "I'm sorry the Brothers Malone are so dreadful. They're almost finished."

As if to prove his point, one of the Brothers Malone dropped his slapstick, hauled a soda-water syphon out of his baggy pants, and chased the other one offstage, squirting at him, as the orchestra gave them a rousing send-off. A couple of folk in the audience even clapped their hands.

Then a young gal in a rainy-suzie spangled skirt came on stage to change the cards on the easel set up to one side.

She got more applause, in one minute, than the Brothers Malone likely had since they'd first come west.

The new card announced the act of Fata Morgana and Company, and the orchestra commenced to play sort of spooky oriental music as a gal sitting center-stage in a harem outfit on a magic carpet slowly rose, carpet and all, to thundergast the audience. As she hovered in midair with the limelight centered on her, two other gals dressed even more shocking ran out from the wings with a long length of red silk stretched between. They kept running as they passed the silk over the hovering gal to show her carpet wasn't suspended on wires. She made snaky movements with her bare arms and tore after them on her flying carpet as yet another gal tore out the other way to do cartwheels as the limelight followed her in turn. Longarm yawned as, at his side, Susan gasped and said, "Now that was pretty good. How do you suppose she made her carpet fly like that?"

He said, "Easy. They got a sheet of plywood under it to keep it flat. She had her waist through a hole in said plywood. The legs crossed atop the carpet were fake. Her real legs were in black tights. All she had to do was stand up and run offstage before anyone wondered why nobody passed silk *under* her on a half-dark stage."

The woman sharing the box with him gaped at him in wonder and asked, "How did you know that? You told me on the train you were a lawman, not a magician."

He shrugged and said, "I've been studying the subject more than most, of late. Once you know there's no such thing as real magic, you sort of get the hang of it. Touring magic shows have to keep their tricks simple. Theatres just don't have all the secret trapdoors and overhead cranes the audience is watching for. Let's see what they do next."

Fata Morgana and her troupe mostly waved silk streamers about, as far as he could tell. The streamers kept changing colors and it was hard to judge how many were in the act, let alone where half those streamers

178

were coming from or going to. Longarm had to agree it was a run-of-the-mill show for a small-time show house. He was pretty sure he'd never made love to any of those three, or was it four gals, by the time he'd watched them flash their silk-clad figures all over creation without really doing much. Then, as if they too sensed it was about time to do something to top that first trick with the magic carpet, they dragged two big boxes, painted red and gold, out from either wing. As two of 'em picked up one box to tilt toward the audience—as if it was as empty as it looked—Longarm nodded, folded his program into a paper glider, and let fly.

As the silly-looking creation swooped back and forth above the audience, some looked up and laughed while others yelled to cut it out and give the little ladies a chance. Longarm leaned back, satisfied, as his paper glider made it as far as the orchestra pit and vanished. Susan stared at him as if he'd just suggested something disgusting and asked him why he was acting so silly. He said, "Misdirection. I was taught by the Great Costello never to make an expected move when you can manage another."

She said, "Well, I certainly never expected a grown man to pull a kid stunt like that. Oh, look, one of those harem girls is climbing into a box."

He said, "I know. She had no way of knowing the Great Costello bragged to me about that trick. I reckon they feel it's a good trick as well. But let's see how *my* trick works."

Before she could ask him what he meant, two uniformed Denver coppers stepped out on stage to sit firmly on the lids of both magic boxes. Others were coming on stage as the curtain suddenly dropped, so the audience didn't get to catch the rest of Longarm's own stage illusion, and booed accordingly.

Susan started to rise, saying, "Let's get out of here. I fear you've started a riot."

But he hauled her back down and soothed, "No sense

getting trampled on the stairs. Denver P.D. and the other federal deputies I invited to the show can control the crowd without our help. What was that shocking sex act you were saving up for later, honey? I've always been a curious cuss and we got plenty of time to talk as we wait for things to simmer down."

She laughed, wildly, and said, "I was looking for adventure, not a police raid, when I picked you up, you goof!"

Then Deputy Guilfoyle parted the curtains of their box and stuck his face in, grinning, to say, "We got five of 'em—the four onstage and the one lurking offstage as their manager. Her hair ain't red no more, but otherwise she answers to your description of the one twin daughter, Maureen. I'm sure glad old Dutch grabbed the one I met at the hotel that time. She keeps yelling rape and Dutch never done a thing but handcuff her."

"I hope you searched the dressing rooms like I said," Longarm said.

"I did. Found another sheet of them special delivery stamps, but not much cash. That wicked twin is still at large, so she likely has it."

Longarm sighed and said, "I was afraid of that. They used the cash from that stamp transaction to buy the new props they just showed off. They had to do something honest-looking while they waited for big sister to get here with the real money."

Guilfoyle asked, "Don't you mean the twin to the one we just caught?"

"I thought I did. Costello never denied it, and I jumped to conclusions. I figured they worked that magic box trick with twins. But as you just saw, two gals in the same wigs and outfits are close enough. Costello never saw fit to point out that, like everyone else trying to figure a magic trick, I made it more complicated than it really needed to be. It was dumb of me to conclude Maureen was the boss sister when Costello swapped his fool self for her. As soon as you study on it you can see a fond parent would value *all* his daughters. It would have been dumb of Costello to entrust the loot to a daughter the law knew anything about, and Maureen got to know me in the biblical sense when she picked me up to keep an eye on me the night before the big Denver bust-out.''

Guilfoyle grinned sheepishly and said, "Oh, I forgot to tell you. The gal who picked me up in the taproom that night was the one who rides magic carpets a lot. That's why I got Dutch to arrest her."

Longarm nodded and said, "Smart move. The only one left for any of us to arrest is the one who stayed well out of the picture. The one entrusted with the money. Knowing the way the Great Costello thought, I'm betting she didn't travel with 'em and made sure she stayed in other hotels in other parts of town as they traveled."

Susan had of course been listening all this time, but seemed to find it all distasteful as well as confusing. She rose to her feet and said, "The crowd down there has thinned out enough for us to leave. Or would you rather stay a while? I could meet you at my place, later."

Longarm said, "Hold the thought, honey. I'm just about done here and I don't want you on the streets without no escort."

She started to protest. Then Billy Vail joined them to announce, "Well, Longarm, I'll allow I thought it was a wild shot, and the judge who issued the search warrant thought it was even wilder. But when you're right, you're right."

Then he held up an all-too-familiar sample case and, as Susan gasped in dismay and Longarm sighed in resignation, Vail continued. "We found this in the hotel room you intimated we might. It sure was heavy, like you said, for a case packed with frilly female notions. That was because of all the silver certificates in high denominations packed in under the false bottom, of course."

All three lawmen in the box turned to Susan to see

181

what she might have to say about the luggage Longarm had carried to her hotel for her, earlier. But she didn't say a word. She turned to grab the railing of the box and vault gracefully over it before anyone could stop her.

She almost made it. She landed feet-first on a seat far below. Then the seat folded under her. She crashed down, face up, to snap her spine on the upright backs of the seats one row closer to the stage. They could hear the ghastly crackle of her parting vertebrae, then her body crumpled down between the seats in a series of dull thuds. Then it got very quiet.

Longarm broke the silence by muttering, "Aw, she didn't have to do that. All we had on her for certain was aiding and abetting. But I noticed on the train, coming up from El Paso, that she was sort of excitable."

Some Denver lawmen were moving toward the dead girl down there, now. Vail said, "I never heard that remark about anyone coming excited on any train, official. But for my own informal curiosity, would someone please tell me how a gal could get that passionate with a lawman who'd just shot it out with her own father, and won?"

Longarm shrugged and said, "Desperation. Knowing I was a lawman still searching for her friends and relations must have excited her more than any desire for revenge and, well, you know what they say about love and hate being close kin. She picked me up to find out how close I might be to figuring the whole deal out. It was a trick she'd either taught or learned from her kid sister, and I have to confess it almost worked on me a second time. Ain't us men fools when it comes to nice-looking women?"

Guilfoyle sighed and said, "I've noticed that, myself. But how did you get on to her, pard?"

Longarm said, "I didn't, until I'd been on her a spell. It's a shuddersome thing to study on. I even went to sleep a few winks, with her and my guns in the same compartment. I wasn't thinking all that much about

182

members of the gang at large until Billy told me some of 'em at least were in Denver."

He reached absently for a smoke as he continued, "Once I knew that, and that the early arrivals had to be strapped for cash if they were cashing in stamps so risky, I started thinking again."

He lit his cheroot and explained, "I recalled how heavy that one sample case had been, and that reminded me that I'd have had a time meeting any gal aboard that train from El Paso if she hadn't been in El Paso about the time I was shooting it out with the last male members of the gang. I was still hoping she just admired my shoulders as much as she let on, but I thought it only common sense to wire the outfit she said she sold stuff for and, guess what, she'd been fibbing about that. She knew a lot of show business terms for a traveling saleswoman. But, like I said, we'd have never convicted her all that serious if she hadn't kept acting so wild to the end."

He turned to Vail to ask, "Do you reckon her sisters in sin will get off light, seeing we recovered the money and all?"

Billy Vail said, "I doubt any of the others will have to serve much time. I don't want either of you two to testify how any of 'em might have served you!"

All three had to laugh. Then Guilfoyle said, "It was mean of them to poison me like that. But I have to admit that this time the law came out ahead, in more ways than one."

Watch for

LONGARM ON THE THUNDERBIRD RUN

one hundred and eleventh novel in the bold
LONGARM series from Jove

coming in March!